MW01148885

This is a work of fiction which is inspired, in part, by historic events. Names, characters, and incidents either are a product of the author's imagination or are used fictitiously. Any resemblance to actual persons, living or dead is entirely coincidental.

ISBN-13: 978-1983237850
ISBN-10: 1643166875

Morals Clause

A novel by John E. Riddle

1

● ● ● ● ● ● ● ● ● ● ● ● ● ●

Fairbanks Ranch, Southern California

I was running along the dark, wind-swept beach when I felt the cold, steel blade rip into my shoulder, driving me headfirst into the wet sand. The pain was excruciating, and within seconds, my body was burning up and drowning in its own blood and sweat. Panic overtook me, and I felt myself straining for my next breath of air. When I tried to get up, I could feel the claustrophobic shrouds of something wet holding me down.

Within seconds or maybe minutes, who knew when I was in this state of mind, I ripped away from the clinging, damp restraints and suddenly was wide awake.

As usual, I found my tangled bedsheets wrapped around my legs, my body dripping wet with sweat.

I glanced towards the digital clock on my nightstand and noticed that it was a blurry 3:33 a.m. I stared at the numbers until they became readable. My eyeballs felt like they were coated with a fine-grit sandpaper. I blinked my eyes a few times to try and get some moisture in them.

When I awake like this, I always try to remain very still while I slowly wait for my eyes to function enough to see if I was in any immediate danger. A quick glance informed me that I was still probably alone in my room.

My heart was beating faster than usual, as I swung my legs off the bed and onto the soft carpeted floor.

While still sitting on the side of the bed, in the pitch dark, I listened carefully to the sounds of the room and the house beyond. It is amazing how many little creaking sounds you can hear in a large house. I really don't need a home this big anymore.

Unlike people who are afraid of the dark and like to keep a few lights on, during the night, I am the exact opposite. I love it absolutely dark. If I can't see them, they can't see me. I listened for a few more seconds and heard absolutely nothing or almost nothing.

I pushed the light function on my iPhone. The piercing brightness diffused the darkness and made everything in the room freeze into place in various hues of stark grays and absolute blacks.

I looked carefully around the room. Nothing seemed to be out of place or unusual. I glanced back towards the bed and quickly turned away.

I opened the drawer beneath the clock, removed a dark, colored gun---a Kimber, Tactical Pro II weighing nearly 2 lbs., and moved slowly towards the nearby window. There was no need to check to see if it was loaded, cocked, and ready to fire. I did that task every night before lights-out.

After carefully parting the drapes, I looked out over the front lawn below. The sprinklers had just turned on, and they were making their usual clacking sounds, in quiet Fairbanks Ranch.

I moved away from the window and crossed the room to view the security display panel. I saw that it was rhythmically blinking a frenetic, red light, indicating it was both armed and ready and had not been disturbed or bypassed.

My heart was now slowly beating in my chest again. This type of disrupted sleep wasn't an unusual occurrence for me. In fact, it happens quite often.

My friends and associates have told me that it is time for me to resume my life again, but I find that's easier said than done.

Everybody, it seems, read about me in the newspapers and on the internet. You name it, from the London Times to the Wall Street Journal, and of course, my local San Diego Union, they all reported the results of the trial.

The funny thing about the mainstream media is that they usually only touch the surface of what they sensationally report.

There have to be a dozen songs about *reading between the lines*---well no one has done that, as yet, about my life. The stuff between the lines could fill the pages of several books. They might read like fiction, but believe or not, every page would be true.

What keeps me awake at night and as cautious as a cat walking around rocking chairs during the day? It is the stuff that they didn't report or weren't allowed to publish.

Don't believe everything that you read, even if you were a former friend of mine. A lot was going on that you're never going to find out about, especially from the media.

I glanced again over at the bed and wished that I could just lay down and go back to sleep.

Typically, I would be getting up in an hour or two to start another day. It would be a day of trusting no one, checking every shadow for trouble, and watching the rearview mirror for unwanted associates from days gone past.

I slipped on some running shorts and a t-shirt and made my way downstairs, as quietly as possible. Not *quiet* to surprise possible bad guys, but quiet so that I didn't wake my favorite son, who usually can sleep through anything. On my way downstairs, I opened his door a few inches and saw that he was lost in a dream world. I could play drums in his room, and he wouldn't hear me.

I chose a half and half pack and placed it in my Keurig, and brewed my first cup of java for the day.

I'm not going to find any lasting relief until I tell someone what really happened. The shrinks have said to me that if I can get it out in the open and share it with friends---I would probably feel a lot better about myself. I don't believe in shrinks because they've let me down in the past. Someone once told me that shrinks have one of the highest suicide rates of any profession. They don't seem to be able to deal with their own problems. As I said, there is not a lot of trust there. I'd prefer to try to handle my issues myself.

If I'm wrong, what's the worst that could happen? Lose a little sleep or get a bullet in the back? Stranger things have happened.

Let's see, I have plenty of coffee and the morning is young, and I don't expect any interruptions for at least a couple of hours. So maybe I should tell my story.

So how bad was it? Well, to start, I still carry at least one concealed weapon on me wherever I go. The Kimber that I'm still holding in my hand is just one of several guns

I own and maintain on a steady basis. I never know when I'm going to need them.

It was terrible enough to distrust even some of my closest friends. I need to correct myself. I can only count on two friends, Jenny and my fifteen-year-old son, Mikey. My son is currently attending our local private prep school a few blocks away from our home.

Other than those two, I don't claim to have any close friends. The others might think we're close, but we're not. How could I trust anyone after the shit I was drowning in? Friends and business partners were my downfall. I won't ever forget. And, by now, it's apparent, they won't forget me either.

2

· · · · · · · · · · · · · · ·

Sam is who I am

My name is Sam Barns, and I am what they call a serial entrepreneur---Or, probably more accurately, a serial, paranoid entrepreneur.

As an entrepreneur, I sometimes start a new business and work with it until it hopefully becomes profitable, then I hustle like a madman to try and find potential buyers. When I get to this point, I need to be able to read the potential buyers like a book. The keyword here is *buyers*. A buyer will pay me less than *buyers* will. I have to create a scenario whereby at least two parties are competing against each other to purchase my business.

When two parties compete, the cost formulas disappear, causing the value of the company to increase exponentially. Instead of offering me a multiple of my annual sales volume or net profit, I make sure that they also have to consider other essential factors. Factors, such as intellectual property rights, unique branding opportunities and the most important of all, Mojo.

Yes, I admit it, Mojo. The world learned about the importance of Mojo while watching Austin Powers lose and then regain his in his highly acclaimed series of movies.

Mojo is the secret sauce of a business transaction.

So what is mojo? It is the unsaid promises of a business transaction. It is the area of your business that adds intrinsic value to your buyer.

After thoroughly investigating potential buyers, I have a pretty good idea of what they are financially worth, what they can afford, and whether or not they are reliable potential buyers. I try to find out every tidbit of information that I can about their businesses---such as what problems they are currently having, and what they need to accomplish in the future to meet their growth projections. By knowing this type of information, I can often add complimentary mojo services that might add value to the deal. The buyer evaluates my company to determine how it will satisfy his current and future needs even though he is making offers to me based on straight book value.

At this point, he is not aware that I often know more about his business than most of his top management. I will then tell him about some additional capabilities that we have been exploring.

If these additional capabilities could tie in with other technologies that he is already using, he might determine there is a higher value to my company. If I can get a competitive bidder to feel the same way, they can outbid each other until I select a lucky winner.

By now, most people have heard of cloud technology. If you were to ask ten computer nerds to explain cloud technology, you would probably get ten different answers.

Mojo is like that. Mojo is a hint of something special in a business deal that everyone can get a whiff of, but nobody can exactly put their fingers on it. It is a mystical cloud of good things to come in a business transaction. Build up the mojo, and the price of your company grows along with it.

This whole process of building up a company and then hand-selecting the perfect buyout partner is a precarious business. If you do it wrong, you can lose everything. If you do right, you can *sometimes* lose everything.

I started to fully understand the seriousness of such a risk when I sold my last company.

What was my first clue? Was it when people tried to kill me? Stab me in my back with a knife? Shoot me with a gun? Or, was it when they tried to steal me blind, thinking I was a young, inexperienced businessman who could be coerced and blackmailed into not fighting back and making a quick surrender?

Yeah, being an entrepreneur is risky, all right. All of the above and more have happened to me, but very few of my acquaintances have heard any of the details, and those who did, probably thought I was exaggerating, or just downright lying. Maybe it's time for people to decide for themselves.

3

• • • • • • • • • • • • • •

In the beginning

Seven years ago, I had started a small business in the resort and travel industry. What could be more peaceful than luxury resorts and first-class travel?

Thanks to a BS degree from SDSU and an MBA from Stanford, with an emphasis in information technology, I was ready to revolutionize a segment of the way people vacation.

Leisure Pathways Technologies (Leisure PT) was a fun opportunity to visit exotic places all over the world. My initial business plan summary indicated that the plan was to grow the concept into a great investment opportunity for a future buyout by one of the big players in the hospitality industries.

Admittedly, I felt that I couldn't call myself a serial entrepreneur until I had at least completed three such new companies, and this was to be my third. So I'm calling myself a serial entrepreneur. I've been called worse.

I had a relatively simple formula for achieving success as such an entrepreneur. I always invested a minimum amount of my own money. I was a firm believer in OPM. It was usually best to use *other people's money*, rather than to tie up all of your own capital. When using OPM, it was always a silent OPM. I did not want partners to second-guess me all of the time. It was my risk, and it would be my reward or failure. An investor was merely that. He loaned me the money, and I would pay him back with interest. Nothing more, nothing less. To avoid the need for OPM, I often tried to use sweat equity---my sweat equity. This was one of the advantages of being a better than average programmer with a business mind.

My plan was to build the company as quickly as possible while developing a strong intellectual rights package. With these patents, I could have a robust software platform that could revolutionize the industry, hopefully for years to come.

By the end of three years, before I became too bored with the daily routine of running this particular company, I would attempt to attract key potentials buyers anxious for a buyout.

Leisure PT turned out to be very different from my previous two companies. It was profitable the very first month after I had completed the software. After a few demos, the sales started rolling in.

It was an unusual industry. There were no standard rules to follow on how to run these vast, resort businesses.

Not knowing any better, I decided to make up my own rules, and somewhat ignored those of my competitors.

At first, there were a few problems. The competitors had been in the industry since the introduction of computers to the travel industry. They always competed neck-to-neck, matching rules for rules, turning themselves into clones of each other, separated only by their unique names. The new upstart, Leisure PT, made its own rules and didn't have years of corporate baggage to wade through to cope with the ever-changing industry needs. We entered the industry at a jog, and we were into a dead run after only a few months of business.

I started with only one assistant, and by the end of the fourth month, we had nearly thirty employees. At the end of six months, we had more than one hundred employees. By not knowing or following the prevalent rules, I was able to develop business relationships with most of the major hospitality companies all over the world. We were a huge success.

I felt that we were almost there, but not quite. I was traveling literally all over the world on a monthly basis. My son Mikey had a map of the world, which covered almost one entire wall in his room. He had a large bowl of red stickpins that he used to track me on all of my trips. I was going to have to either get him a larger map, or smaller pins if I didn't stop traveling so much.

"Dad, are you going to be at home this weekend and watch me play in the big AJGA tournament? We're playing at Torrey Pines. I won the first-place trophy in my last tournament. Please, dad!"

"Sorry, I can't, son. I need to be in Hawaii this coming week. Can I get a rain check?" I asked.

My wife, Jenny, caught the tail end of our conversation.

"Sam, can't you take a few days off and enjoy your family. You haven't made it to any of his matches this year. He's doing really good. He sure would like you to see him play. He is really turning into a great golfer." She shook her head towards me and then left the room.

I was getting burned out. I didn't know if I could continue at this pace for another two years before selling the company and moving on. Jenny and Mikey knew I was somehow related to them, but they often didn't see enough of me to believe it.

Just when I needed it, a miracle happened.

Generally, when I was traveling, I would visit at either the resorts or hotels that we were converting over to our software systems or at their corporate headquarters. I worked with their technical staff during the daytime hours and often dined with their upper management in the evenings.

On one particular occasion, I was having dinner with the new CEO of the fourth-largest hotel group in the world. They currently had 400,000 rooms, and like everyone else in the industry, they needed to grow at a faster pace and increase their profits.

I had initially met Brad when he was with his former company, and we had dined frequently together ever since.

Like me, he was in his early thirties, married, and trying to support a young growing family.

After a couple of drinks and a delicious dinner at one of his four-star restaurants, he shared with me some of the stress he was under.

"I should be the happiest guy in the world right now. I've just become one of the youngest CEOs in the hospitality business, working for one of the largest hotel chains in the world. But I'm not. I've never been more stressed out in my life. My income and my career depend on how well I do in this new position. Everyone is expecting me to fail. I will be laughed out of this industry if I can't come up with a new, innovative idea to significantly increase our income levels, or I'll be gone."

I thought about what he had said for a few moments before responding. "What do you have to work with? There are only so many hotel rooms you can build, and you have to spend money to do so. There is only so much you can do to increase room occupancy. Even the best programs would only slightly increase your bottom line. It sounds to me like you need something new and totally innovative. Do you have any ideas?"

Brad shook his head. "No. All the hotel groups are just about in the same boat. We all try to increase revenues by 2% to 3% per year, and we are lucky if we achieve those kinds of numbers. I tell you, I'm up for just about anything that could help me break out of this logjam."

He ordered another dry martini while I continued to sip on a diet coke.

I think a lot better when somebody else drinks my alcohol.

I waited until his drink had arrived, and he had taken a deep swallow.

"I have an idea that would be totally new for your industry. It has to do with a previous business I was involved in. It is really thinking outside the box, but let me get some paper on this, and I'll show you a way to make your revenues go through the roof, and expand your business in a way you may never have thought possible."

Brad summoned the waiter, and within moments he had a notepad and pen placed in front of me.

Later, when Brad had finished his drink, he switched to coffee, and we continued talking for another half hour.

At last, I was through with my impromptu presentation. A newly invigorated Brad rose from the table and gave me an enthusiastic man-hug. "You're the best, Sam. Let's meet first thing in the morning, and I want you to recap what we have discussed with my management team. This could be really great!"

And it was.

4

• • • • • • • • • • • • • •

The birth of a new industry

One of my previous companies had been connected to the timeshare industry. I had started one of the first fully automated exchange companies.

The concept behind timeshares was to initially convert a few condominium units into timeshare units. Each unit was then broken down into a series of weeks that you could own, instead of owning and paying for an entire condominium.

As the industry grew, so did the means of using random condominiums. Larger developers entered the field and began buying and converting older hotels or specifically built small resorts just for timesharing.

Most of the timeshare industry consisted of mom and pop operations. The overall reputation of the industry was questionable at best. Used car salesmen seemed more reputable than the blue suede shoes of a slick timeshare salesman.

My proposal to Brad would change the timeshare and hotel industries forever.

My suggestion was to build compatible timeshare units adjacent to their hotels wherever possible.

The timeshare industry was always battling with credibility issues. Mom and pop operations often could not take care of the rooms properly. They often had problems with their reservation systems. Nothing ingratiates a family more with their favorite timeshare operator than when a family of six shows up for their annual vacation, traveling by car from five states away, only to find out that their room had not been reserved properly.

No problem, there was always next year and another anti-timeshare owner for life.

The idea of buying a timeshare from a hotel chain like a Westin, Hilton or Marriott, took off like a rocket.

The timeshare owners who traded into one of these timeshare resorts could use all of the facilities of the hotels, including their golf courses and restaurants, and they were assured that their reservations would always be honored.

The hotel chains were able to generate an entirely new stream of cash flow. The average cost of building a luxury timeshare room was approximately $200,000. The hotel could sell each room as a timeshare for upwards of $500,000 after dividing it into weeks. The resort could increase their occupancy rates considerably, knowing that timeshare owners almost always used their units each year, or if not, they could trade their unit to someone who would show up. For the hotels, that meant full golf courses, packed restaurants, and lots of people using and paying for all of their amenities.

Leisure PT designed and implemented all of the hardware and software necessary to seamlessly tie the two industries together.

I know it's hard to believe that travel to exotic locations around the globe, could be so devastating on our family.

In the evenings, I would call home after checking into a new hotel from my latest trip. Mikey would ask me what country I was in, and I would have to check my tickets, at times to give him an accurate location. It was getting difficult to maintain my hectic schedules.

I would call my office, back in the United States, before getting on my next flight. I would often be re-directed to a different country at the very last minute. It was all very exhausting.

Jenny was always supportive of my work. She understood that all of my hustle would eventually lead to a significant financial reward for our family, but the lack of a husband was wearing thin for her. To help pass the time and an empty house---and lost days between trips, she threw herself into real estate. Within months she was selling multimillion-dollar properties with the best of them.

Kids are resilient. Mikey's days were full. He was doing great in school and spent any spare time at our local golf course, pounding out golf balls until his arms were tired.

We all could last until my company was positioned to be sold to one of the major companies in the hospitality industry.

5

● ● ● ● ● ● ● ● ● ● ● ● ● ●

Time to go to the market

Within a year, Brad's hotel group had become the darling of the hospitality industry. A short time later, Leisure PT was approached and contracted with three more of the largest hotel groups in the world.

So here I was traveling all over the world, each and every month, staying at some of the world's finest hotels for free. I had long ago integrated most of the world's top airlines into an advanced reservation system, which tied in to all of the hotel groups. Because of this, all of my air travel was first class and free.

Back in our office in San Diego, the phones started ringing off the hooks, and investment bankers were camping out in our lobby. Everyone wanted us to go public. IPO fever was catching everyone's attention.

Rather than spend at least a year and millions of dollars to prepare for an IPO, I began re-evaluating my alternatives.

My buddy, Brad, was interviewed, resulting in a very complimentary article about Leisure PT in Forbes.

Within days, the hospitality industry was approaching me in earnest.

After an additional couple of months, while I did some initial due diligence, I had two major public companies vying for our acquisition.

It was time for a meet and greet.

Southern Industries (SI) was a Fortune 500 conglomerate listed on the New York Stock Exchange. With $12 billion in annual sales revenue and a chairman, Jack Blackwell, who was personally worth well over $1 billion, I was anxious to meet with him.

He sent Southern's private jet to pick me in San Diego, and I flew to Houston to meet with him and his management team. I'll have to admit I was very impressed.

Blackwell was exceptionally well dressed and well mannered. He was a complete gentleman.

After a brief meeting at his headquarters, Blackwell, a lawyer by the name of Thomas McKnight and I, caught a company limo, and a few minutes later, we were seated in the ultra-luxurious, as well as ultra-private, Cattlemen's Club of Houston.

The Cattlemen's Club personified money. The walls and ceiling were all finished in the most luxurious woods imaginable. Even with the subdued lighting, the shiny brass hardware was evident everywhere. It looked like a movie set for the TV show Dynasty.

I was reminded that we were in Texas when the floor manager collected guns from those present as they entered the room. Those who were carrying received a receipt for their weapon.

After an enthusiastic greeting by the maître d', followed by an effusive huddle with a world-renowned chef, we were treated like royalty to a fabulous meal.

The following morning Blackwell greeted me briefly and then invited in his staff, which he directed to complete the acquisition.

I was a bit surprised. He was moving much too fast for me. I explained to him that I still had to meet with another company the following day before I could make an informed decision.

His careful manners failed for a moment, and he tried to hold his temper in place. "What do you mean you are still considering another party? I thought we were the only company you were considering."

"I have to apologize if you got that impression from me. I thought that we were still at an early stage in the negotiations. We have not discussed terms, conditions, or pricing as yet. It would be irresponsible of me to proceed any further without such information."

Blackwell's face seemed to turn slightly red as he shook his head. "You mean you have not received our term sheet as yet?"

I shook my head.

"You have not talked to Tom McKnight before arriving here in Texas?"

I shook my head again. "The first time that I have ever talked to Tom was last night at dinner."

Blackwell excused himself and then stormed out of the room. A few minutes later, he returned with a chagrinned McKnight.

"I have to apologize, Sam. I thought everything had been handled. If you still feel you need to meet with that other party, I fully understand, although I hope that you realize we are the most successful company in this industry. I assure you we can beat any offer that they might put on the table. Who is this other company?" Blackwell asked.

"I'm not at liberty to say, at this time," I responded. "I assured them that their identity would remain private, and I will make that same assurance to you. I can tell you, though, that they are also a public company. I can also tell you that they understand our company quite well and feel that several of our technologies and relationships could be beneficial to them now and in the future."

Blackwell stood there quietly, still staring at McKnight. "Tom, you need to get this done. Whatever it takes." Looking over at me, he continued. "I'm sorry about this miscommunication. That usually doesn't happen around here. Please stay in touch. We want to complete this deal as soon as possible. Call me anytime you have questions about anything. Thanks for visiting with us."

6

• • • • • • • • • • • • • •

When buyers compete,
the price goes up

The next day I flew to Las Vegas in a private Gulfstream G280, owned personally by the chairman of United Resorts International.

Terry Jones owned several of the world's grandest hotels and casinos. After the gratuitous limo pick-up at the airport, I met with the man himself.

He was a complete contrast to Jack Blackwell. While Jack lived in Texas, one of the cowboy capitals of the world, and dressed in $5000 business suits, Jones dressed in cowboy-casual and acted like one of the boys.

We spent the early evening eating at a private restaurant located on the top floor of one of his luxury hotels along the strip. We were the only two customers in the restaurant, while more than a dozen employees served us a delicious meal.

Terry asked me several detailed questions, which I tried to patiently explain to him, but I could tell he wasn't following some of the technologies. He said he had several experts on his staff, who were anxious to work with me.

After dinner, we went down to one of his raucous casinos and tried our luck at the gaming tables. The constant commotion blocked out everything but his loudest comments. He laughed when I kept asking him to speak louder above the crowds and the noise. He slid several stacks of one hundred dollar chips in front of me and slapped me on the back. "Come on, let's have some fun. We can talk later," he yelled as he grabbed two seats for us at a high rollers table.

I returned to my suite at an early 1 a.m. That is an early hour for Las Vegas, which is usually just coming alive at that time of the morning.

I showered and jumped into bed, anxious to get a good night's sleep before meeting with him again in a few hours.

Before I could close my eyes, there was a light tapping on my door. I thought that perhaps Terry had sent up a bottle of champagne or maybe a light snack before I turned in.

I opened the door. It was a light *snack* all right, holding a bottle of Louis Roederer Cristal Brut in her left hand and two crystal glasses in her right.

"Mr. Jones thought that you might like a little company during your visit here in Sin City," she said with oozing sexuality. She smiled as she slithered her way into my room.

We talked for several minutes while I tried to get her to leave. I told her I was a very happily married man. She responded that she bet I was. When she asked if I would prefer some male company, I almost threw her off the balcony.

She explained that she provided specialized services for Mr. Jones. She had been in Las Vegas for the last twelve months and had never been turned down by any prospective client, male or female. TMI.

We finally made a deal. She would get paid from Jones, and I would get a good night's sleep. We would both pretend we had a great time.

When she left, I checked the room from the carpet to the ceiling for recording devices or cameras.

My amateurish search yielded nothing.

7

● ● ● ● ● ● ● ● ● ● ● ● ● ● ●

Add in a little Mojo

The next day I met with Terry and his staff, and it was a productive day. His people were very interested in our programs and services, and Terry made it abundantly clear that he wanted to do the deal.

During a mid-morning break, I had a chance to check on my email and phone messages. There was a term sheet from Blackwell.

At the end of the day, we met back in Terry's office for a final chat. Without beating around the bush, he offered me several million dollars in cash and a bunch of his AMEX traded stock. He also indicated that several perks that went with the job, and then he winked at me and laughed. Hmm.

I thanked him and said I would get back to him in the next couple of days after I had a chance to evaluate his offer.

The next day I called Jack Blackwell at Southern and told him that I appreciated his term sheet but that it didn't approach the value of his competition. After a brief silence, he said he would send me a revised term sheet and then hung up.

Thirty minutes later, I received a new term sheet from Blackwell. He offered more upfront cash than United, but less stock. He asked me to call him immediately if his offer wasn't sufficient.

I called him back and told him that while I appreciated his generous offer, his competitor was also a public company. Their offer of stock was significantly better---millions of dollars better. I tried to reinforce the fact that I preferred selling to Southern, but that there was just too much stock being left off the table to make it a good business decision for me.

Blackwell was silent for so long that I finally asked if he was still on the line. He said that he was and that he would get back to me within an hour with their final offer.

About an hour and a half later, I received a new email from Blackwell. I received an additional million dollars in up-front cash, and an investment account full of Southern preferred stock. The preferred stock could be converted to tradable common stock at any time after 90 days. At the current value of the common stock, I was receiving several more $millions in stock.

True to his word, Blackwell had reworked his final numbers. He offered more upfront cash than United and more in preferred, convertible stock. I was also appointed to seats on two different boards of directors.

The one negative aspect of the deal, I had already anticipated from both parties. I had to agree to a three-year management contract, and my final compensation would be based on an earn-out. That basically meant that if Leisure PT continued to be successful, from a profit standpoint, I could make a lot more money.

Millions more.

If Southern didn't support my programs, the company could suffer, and I, in turn, could lose a lot of potential income. Obviously, it was an opportunity for me to make several additional millions. All I had to do was trust that Southern would support me as promised and understand that we would both make substantial money if we continued to grow and be successful.

If I couldn't trust a Fortune 500 Company---who could I trust?

Southern felt that they needed me to be involved in the daily operations of the company, because of the secret knowledge that I held between my ears, maybe an over calculation on their behalf. I thought I was using common sense, but to them, it was a mystery.

I informed Terry, at United Resorts, of my decision. Although disappointed, he congratulated me and wished me the best of success.

During the next two weeks, the attorneys completed the acquisition paperwork, and Southern signed off on the terms of my employment contract.

They sent their corporate jet to pick up my attorney and me and flew us back to Houston for the closing ceremony.

The *closing ceremony* was the business way of executing a room full of documents that had been previously agreed upon during the past few months of negotiations; it was more of a formality than anything else. It was usually considered the quiet before the storm. Everyone was on his or her best behavior. It was an opportunity to meet fellow members of the board and the members of their upper management before any problems or personality conflicts were discovered.

Four of Southern's top management team, including Blackwell, took us to a celebratory dinner at a local four-star restaurant.

Blackwell was back to his gracious self again and was very pleasant, but slightly distracted throughout the dinner. The only unusual event occurred when my attorney mentioned that he was sorry he did not have an opportunity to meet with Tom McKnight after working with him over the past couple of weeks. Blackwell nodded his head and smiled and then looked away from us and started talking with one of his vice presidents while another division head, mentioned that McKnight was no longer with the company. He had been offered another position, and it was just too good of an opportunity for him to turn down.

We spent the night in one of their luxury hotels and returned to San Diego the following day.

That weekend my family and I celebrated with a trip to Sea World, and the following day was spent at The Wild Animal Park. It was the first time in several months that we had spent two days together. Jenny and Mikey were the happiest I had seen them I years.

On Sunday night I asked the nanny to watch Mikey while Jenny and I went car shopping.

Jenny was in real estate. She spent long hours working with her clients almost every day. After depositing my acquisition check from Southern, I made the assumption that everyone who could drive, in our family, deserved a new car.

We went up to Car Country, in North County San Diego, and stopped at a Mercedes dealer. Within minutes Jenny fell in love with a white S600 Mercedes, and we purchased it for cash.

While Jenny was completing the paperwork, I went next door to the Porsche dealership and purchased a Guards Red Turbo Porsche.

Thirty minutes later, we were chasing each other, playing tag with our new toys, all of the way home.

8

● ● ● ● ● ● ● ● ● ● ● ● ● ● ●

Leisure PT and Colonel Sanders

The following Monday, I arrived early at our offices back in San Diego. The building looked the same, but from here on out, I would be working for a Fortune 500 company, and not paying for everything out of my own pocket. I could feel any remains of financial stress leave my body as I pulled up to our building in my gleaming new Porsche.

To my surprise, I found Colonel Sanders, with a bucket full of Buffalo wings tucked under one of his arms, waiting for me on my front doorstep.

It wasn't really the Colonel, but it could have been his doppelganger.

He introduced himself as Randall (not Randy) Pate. He looked to be chronologically in his early fifties, but physically in his late sixties. He was wearing a three-piece, gray pinstriped suit, which without too much imagination, I assumed had been purchased on Savile Row in London. Randall appeared to be a very successful businessman.

The only characteristics that seemed to detract from his overall image of affluence and prosperity, was an age disparity. A significant network of small, red capillaries covered his nose and cheeks, and there was of course, a paunch at his midriff that could only be attributed to being well fed or over-indulgent.

After a brief introduction, I guided him into my office, and we sat down at my desk.

"I hope this isn't too much of an imposition for you," said Randall as he paused and smiled smugly. "Jack and Clem have asked me to act as their eyes and ears out here in California. They want us to basically become very close business associates so that we can better integrate our two companies together. They need to understand exactly what you do and how you do it. They want to be assured that they did not buy a pig in a poke," he said with a grimace. "They need to know precisely what Southern has acquired."

It took me less than a few seconds to understand what was happening. They had purchased my company, and now they needed to figure out the value of my Mojo. Was it qualitative or quantitative? Had extra dollars had been spent due to their own exuberance to make a much-needed purchase?

Either they had not reviewed my purchase agreement and employment contract, or they were just starting to play the role of a large Fortune 500 Company. Maybe I was reading too much into this, but I felt that I needed to go down on the record with a few comments.

I looked thoughtfully at Randall for a moment before speaking. "Jack, being Jack Blackwell, the Chairman of the Board of SI?" I asked, already knowing the answer. "And, Clem---who's that?"

"That's Clem Garland from our southeastern division. He runs WRI. You know Western Resorts International. You need anything done---you just ask for Clem. Everybody calls him that except the rank and file employees, of course."

I nodded my head but needed more clarification. "I have to get something straight with you. Three days ago, I signed contracts with SI in Houston. In those contracts, I was legally assured that I would be running the leisure division, with minimal supervision. It doesn't sound like it if you are expecting to be literally looking over my shoulder every day while I'm trying to build this company."

Randall silently raised one of his hands as if solemnly trying to interrupt me. "Sam, please let's not get off on the wrong foot here, this early in our relationship. I don't want you to think that I'm here, *at Jack's request*, to spy or tie your hands behind your back," he shook his head vigorously. "Jack wants me to facilitate anything you need to kick this little company into high gear so that you can take it and run with it. As you've probably been told, Southern has twenty-three separate business divisions and is made up of nearly seventy different corporations all folded up under one big family umbrella. We own large hotel chains, luxurious casinos, and huge resort communities. everything from gambling casinos to huge resort communities. We own the largest mass marketing company in the United States. We have a banking division. We even have our own small airline," he paused for a moment to re-enforce the look of pure honesty still apparent on his face. "They want to share all of these assets with you. It takes someone that has been with the company for years to understand everything that might be available to you---so that you can use them for the betterment of your company."

"Okay, I can understand that, but how close of a business associate are you supposed to become?"

Randall vigorously nodded his head. "Jack has asked me to only to hang out with you. I'm going to get an apartment here in San Diego, get a car and be your sidekick on all of your business trips, just until we can get a handle on all of the nuances of your business," he paused again and then looked directly into my eyes. "That is, of course, if you are willing to let me tag along. All of my expenses will be billed to another division, so you don't have to worry about those costs. Believe me---I'm not going to say a word in meetings unless you direct me to do so."

I looked at him skeptically.

"As an example, we have sophisticated overnight banking capabilities that can increase cash flow and add to profitability. By sweeping everyone's bank accounts every twenty-four hours, we can ensure that we receive the maximum use of our money. But, until I know your needs, I can't be of much help to you."

"You referenced my company as a pig in a poke. Really? I don't know what is worst, calling my company that name, or working for a company that just paid a small fortune for it. I think you can appreciate my dilemma."

Randall looked nervous for a moment. "Sam, that was just a figure of speech---an ill-advised figure of speech."

I stared into space for a few seconds. "Randall, could you give me the room for a moment. I need to make a couple of phone calls, and then I will get right back to you."

Randall looked nervous as he exited the room.

I called Blackwell, and he answered immediately. I voiced my concerns about my autonomy and my visit from Randall Pate. He told me that from a company structural standpoint, my leisure division reported through Western Resorts International, which was run by Clem Garland. He had asked Clem to try and make an effort to find out how Leisure PT was so successful. The assignment of Randall to California had been his decision, at his cost, and he would appreciate it if I would at least give it a try.

After a brief hesitation, I told him I would.

I called Randall back into my office. "Well, welcome aboard, Randall. Make yourself at home. I'm sure we will all benefit from your experience. By the way, I'm leaving tomorrow morning for Hong Kong. Is your passport up to date? If you want to tag along, you're certainly welcome."

~ ~***~ ~

Early the next morning, I had a taxi drop me off at the curb at Lindbergh Field. I was wearing jeans, a T-shirt, and a light leather jacket.

As the taxi driver was removing my bag from his trunk, a stretch limo glided to halt, taking up two lanes in the parking area behind us. I vaguely wondered what superstar wannabe would exit the vehicle.

Without spending any more time, I paid my driver, grabbed my carry-on, and headed towards the large glass entry doors leading into the terminal. I felt a nudge from behind as a porter brushed by me trying, to wrestle two massive Louis Vuitton suitcases towards the check-in counter. Another porter, with two more pieces of matching luggage, followed close behind. Bringing up the rear of this flamboyant tag team was Randall.

Randall was wearing a different three-piece business suit this morning. Perhaps he didn't realize the trip would take more than eighteen hours of sitting in a cramped airplane. While I had packed a carry-on suit bag with all my clothes in it, Randall had checked-in with four full-size suitcases.

He turned out to be a better traveler than I expected.

As the wheels lifted off the runway, he pushed the call button above his seat. A few minutes later, when it was safe to move around the cabin, the hostess came over to him.

"How may I help you, sir?" She asked politely.

"I think my associate and I could use a drink about now," Randall replied.

She smiled but didn't bother to look at her watch. The sun was barely up. "What can I get for you?"

"I would like Absolut, straight up," he paused and looked over at me. "How about it, Sam---shall we make it two?"

"No thanks, I think I'll have an orange juice, for the time being."

We changed planes in Los Angeles and continued on towards Hong Kong.

During the next couple of hours, Randall ingratiated himself with a new stewardess while consuming another six or so vodkas and was deep asleep before lunch was served. He slept like a dead man all the way to China.

As we exited the airplane and headed down the terminal towards the passport control. Randall stumbled ahead and grabbed the arm of the stewardess who had been feeding him drinks during the flight. He whispered in her ear for several seconds while she tried desperately to pull away. He finally passed her a piece of paper and let go of her arm. She quickly ran off towards the elevators.

He caught up with me again and smiled. "Well, you can't expect a guy not to ask for the order. She was flirting with me the entire flight. I told her to call me after she got settled. We'll see. Maybe she'll call or maybe she won't. You'll never know unless you ask for the order."

Oh, this was going to be a long trip.

It was my practice, while on such business trips, to move fast and to fill every day with appointments so that I could leave town and get back home all that much sooner.

I had reservations for us at the Regent Hotel in Kowloon. It was considered one of the better hotels in Hong Kong, on the mainland side, situated oceanfront with unobstructed views of the harbor towards the island of Hong Kong. Thousands of freighters, pleasure boats, and Chinese junks sailed back and forth across the bay, within a hundred yards from the back of the hotel. Every room had floor to ceiling windows that captured this picture-perfect view. The only things detracting from this exotic local was the pungent odors emanating from the garbage-filled streets and decaying refuse near the wharves. Hong Kong was always hot and humid, and the air just turned into steam as soon as it hit your body.

On our first morning in Hong Kong, I waited downstairs in the restaurant for Randall to join me for our 7 a.m. breakfast. At 7:30 a.m. I called his room. His voicemail picked up, and I told him that I had missed him at breakfast but would see him later that evening if he wanted to get together for dinner.

I spent the day visiting two of our local resorts. When I arrived back at the hotel at around 6 p.m., Randall was sitting in the lobby, sipping a martini and looking nervous while he awaited my arrival.

He explained to me that he had turned off his phone in his room so that he could get some sleep. He indicated that Blackwell had called him several times and that he was exhausted when he finally turned in. He forgot to request a wake-up call. I told him not to worry about it. If he wanted to stay in the hotel all day, that was fine.

I suggested that we walk a couple blocks down the street and have a nice dinner at the Peninsula Hotel, and he readily agreed. Everything was fine until we exited the air-conditioned hotel and started walking together through the sweltering streets of Hong Kong.

At 7 p.m., it was still close to 90 degrees. The humidity was hovering at about 85%. The sweet smell of raw sewage saturated the stagnant air. I pretended like I did not notice that Randall was sweating like a stuffed pig in his three-piece wool suit. I'll have to admit, though, he acted like a trooper and never voiced a complaint until after we had finished our supper and we were ready to head back to our hotel. He rushed passed me as we left the restaurant and snagged a taxi before I was even out to the curb. Randall wasn't about to get hot and sweaty again, at least not tonight.

Back at the hotel, as we entered the lobby, Randall excused himself for a moment, and I watched him as he approached one of the bellhops and whispered a few words in his ear. He passed a few folded up bills to the man and then made his way back over to me.

"What do say, Sam, can we just pass on the after-dinner drinks tonight? I've just arranged for a little in-room entertainment, so, with a little luck, I hope I'm going to be busy for the rest of the evening."

Whatever floats your boat, I thought.

The next morning, he was sipping on a Bloody Mary when I entered the restaurant at 6:55 a.m. He was wearing another new three-piece suit and looked as though he hadn't slept a wink for the last 24 hours, but he was ready to go.

In truth, Randall was not such a bad guy. He was easy to travel with. After a few appointments, in which he would remain absolutely quiet, we would return to the hotel. After a few drinks, he would order a playmate from one of the staff, and I wouldn't see him again until the next morning. The next day after a couple of cocktails for breakfast, I would just point him in whatever direction we needed to travel.

Randall was almost a perfect travel companion.

9

• • • • • • • • • • • • • •

Mississippi Delta

During the following six months, Leisure Pathway Technologies increased sales and profits by more than 500%. We opened three more offices, one in London, and the other two in Barcelona and Brazil. We had become one of the most dominant companies in the resort services industry. Unfortunately, not everyone shared my enthusiasm for our success.

It soon became apparent that even though we all worked for the same company and contributed to its bottom line, there was a lot of jealousy among the various divisions. The more successful our division became, the more unsuccessful other divisions appeared to upper management.

Clem Garland was in charge of SI's resort-oriented subsidiaries. Leisure PT contributed significantly to their success. Structurally, I was supposed to report to Garland on the corporate ladder.

Randall and I were requested to fly to Gautier, (*GO-chay*) Mississippi to meet with Clem Garland for the first time.

It soon became apparent to me that Garland and Randall were close friends. Clem Garland was a down-home country boy who seemed to be as jovial as a patient who had just been told that his herpes test had come back negative. He was almost Randall's opposite.

He presented himself as a self-deprecating, humble, confused lackey of the business world. I had met managers like him before. He was dressed in snazzy golf clothes (if you consider lime green slacks and a burnt orange polo shirt snazzy). A large picture of the thirteenth hole at Augusta covered half the wall in his expansive office. Every square foot of the office space was covered with some type of golf memorabilia, little trophies, pictures of Garland with Chi Chi Rodriques and another dozen or so members of the senior golf tour, plus rack after rack of logoed golf balls purchased from golf shops all around the world.

Garland was also the guy who had forced Randall down my throat, and I had a feeling he was the source of a lot of the jealousy directed towards Leisure PT.

With a psychotic smile on his face and a cigarette hanging dangerously between his lips, Garland jumped around the side of his desk and shook my hand with both of his own. "Damn, it's good to finally meetcha Sam! Sam Barns, imagine that! I'll have to admit I was expecting somebody a lot older."

I wasn't sure how I was supposed to take that.

"Is it just beginners luck, or are you really that good? I'm glad you could break away from your busy schedule to come on down here to meet with us."

He took a few steps towards Randall and shook his hand and then patted him a few times on the shoulder as if to make sure it was really him.

Before I could return his enthusiastic greeting, he made a sweeping gesture with his arms to encompass all of the golf crap in his office.

"Did yawl bring your sticks with ya?" He asked with unconcealed interest.

"We sure did," I said. "Randall and I decided to turn this whole week into one big golf vacation. We can talk about business stuff some other time," I replied with a friendly smile.

Garland looked at me closely. "Really?"

He immediately struck me as one of those individuals who you meet in life that you just don't like during the first contact, or for that matter, any contact after that. I hate cigarette smoke. My father had died in his late forties from lung cancer. I would rather walk out on a great business deal than have to work with a smoker. I'm sure that the fact that he had saddled me with Randall and was the source for all of the jealousy problems with

Leisure PT had nothing to do with my current humor attack.

"No, I'm not serious," I said as I slapped him playfully on his back. "Randall told me that you are one of the best bowlers in this part of the country, and I just assumed that we wouldn't need our golf clubs."

Garland looked confused for a moment and then glanced over towards Randall, who just shrugged his shoulders and looked away.

Before he could get his thoughts together, I took another thrust. I walked over to an old antique leather golf bag leaning against the wall that displayed several old wooden clubs. I selected one of the clubs and waved it out in front of me as if I was trying to get a feel for it. "Are these your clubs? How far can you hit them?"

He took the club out of my hands and placed it reverently back into the bag. "Yes, they're my clubs, but I don't use them. I use a newer set when I actually play."

I touched the club again and then looked back towards him. "Boy, if I owned these clubs, I would play with them all of the time."

"So I take it, you don't play much golf out there on the west coast?"

"Not much," I said. "I was actually pulling your leg earlier. My favorite sport *is* actually bowling. I thought maybe you would like to play."

"Seriously? Bowling is really your sport?"

"Mr. Garland, I'm as serious as lung cancer," I replied confidently. "Bowling is number one in my book, followed by tennis, and then if I have still have enough time, I'll play a little golf. In fact, I bought a really nice set of used Golfcraft clubs about five years ago. Some of the grips have come off, but I still play them from time to time."

He nodded his head vigorously. "That's okay. We can rent ya some newer clubs. Ya know Sam, ya can learn more about a man during eighteen holes of golf than you can during a month worth of business meetings. Besides, we gotta have some fun in our lives," he said as he dug his elbow into Randall's side and laughed.

He paused for a moment, as if deep in thought. "And, remember, my friends all call me Clem."

So, my new friends and I went to play golf.

Garland picked us up in his Lincoln Town Car and reminded us, (primarily me) that it was important to buy American. Randall obviously had told him that I was driving a new Turbo Porsche. Damn those Germans.

We traveled down some back roads, which were bordered with swamps, at more than 90 MPH. He waived dismissingly at a police car that had set up a speed trap along the side of the road.

Without looking up from his driving, he laughed and said, "When ya own the country club, own one of the biggest companies in Mississippi, and most of the people in town work for ya, I'm pretty much allowed to drive as fast as I want."

I had Googled Clem when I first heard his name. He owned just about everything within fifty miles from here. I was surprised that they hadn't change the name of the town to Clem City.

By the time we had reached our destination, Garland was speeding at well over 100 mph and had to brake sharply to avoid crashing into the massive entry gates. Randall looked as though he was ready to lose his breakfast. I think Garland was still trying to impress me with his fiefdom ownership.

The magnolia-lined entry to the Country Club wound its way for nearly a mile until we arrived at a beautiful building that was reminiscent of an old southern plantation.

Nearly a dozen black workers were attending to the outside gardens as we slid up to the building in a spectacular cloud of billowing dust. Garland honked his horn loudly and then waved his hand towards the workers, causing several of them to jump out of the way in fear of being hit. "I don't know what we'd do without the help of our niggas, Sam. Have you got a bunch of them out there in San Diego?"

"Black people?"

"Yeah, niggas."

"I couldn't tell you. We don't really notice that kind of thing. We are right on the border with Mexico. We have a lot of diversity out there."

"So, you got a lot of trouble with the beaners, huh?"

"No, not really," I said with complete sincerity, while thinking---you racist pig. "Some of my best friends are Hispanic."

He looked over at me for a moment to see if I was serious, and then over at Randall, who pointedly looked out the window in a different direction.

~ ~***~ ~

Garland had phoned ahead, and, as we exited his American made car, we were greeted by a fair number of employees from the golf shop. While Garland and the local pro, Chip, were hitting a quick bucket of balls to warm up, Randall and I were outfitted to look like golfers---a more subtle version than Garland.

The staff followed us out to the first tee to watch their employer morph into a young Jack Nicklaus. Garland spent ten minutes or so cracking golf jokes, of which everyone present had probably heard at least a dozen times since they were children.

"Did you hear the one about the wife who thought her husband looked more haggard and disgruntled than usual after his weekly golf game---she asked him what was wrong.

He answered, "Well, on the fourth hole, Harry had a heart attack and died. It was terrible! The entire rest of the day, it was hit the ball, drag Harry, hit the ball, and drag Harry!"

—Forced laughter.

A wife and her husband are sitting around one evening, just talking, when the wife suddenly asks, "If I died, would you re-marry?"

"I would," the husband answered promptly.

"You would?" the wife asked, a bit surprised. "Would you let her come inside my house?"

"I would."

"Would she be cooking in my kitchen?"

"She would!"

"Would she be soaking in my bathtub?"

"She would!"

"Would she be putting her clothes in my closet?"

"She would!"

Growing more exasperated, the wife continued asking: "Would she be driving my car?"

"She would!"

"Would she be sleeping in my bed?"

"She would indeed!"

"Would she be using my golf clubs?"

"Oh, no, definitely not."

"Why not?"

"She's left-handed."

Like dutiful employees everywhere, they laughed hysterically at the punch lines. They also nodded appreciatively as Garland teed up his ball and made a few out-of-control practice swings. Clumps of golf turf flew in every which direction.

Before they needed to rebuild the tee box area, he settled down and approached his ball and took a few precise waggles with the clubhead. Just when everyone was sure he was going to finally make his first real swing, he stopped suddenly and slapped his gloved hand against his forehead and stepped away from his ball.

"Damn, I was so excited about playing golf, I totally forgot to set our bets," he said, smiling like a lunatic. "Let's see, Chip and I will play best-ball against you and Randall. Then let's set up some individual bets." He looked over at his staff, grinning and then over at me. "Sam, I'm just an old hacker, how about you giving me four strokes a side? And Randall, I'll give you two a side."

Randall looked angry for a moment and then shifted his eyes away. "Sure, Clem," he mumbled.

If this were a serious game, I would have laughed out loud. Nobody gives an unknown golfer four strokes a side unless they have played with them before and know for a fact they are not that good of a player.

"Really? Four strokes a side? I give my grandmother three strokes a side, and she also plays with wooden clubs." I paused for a moment as I watched Garland get ready to argue. "Ah, what the hell. It's only money. Four strokes a side is fair enough. I hit some golf balls a few months ago, so I should be warmed up and ready."

There was more than $1000 placed in bets. I watched as Garland started salivating with glee as he rubbed his hands together. He also proposed that we play a game called Bingo, Bango, Bungo---Seriously. Whoever gets their ball on the green first gets paid $5 from each golfer. Whoever is the closest to the pin gets another $5. The first one to get their ball in the hole gets another $5.

As long as you are a CPA and have plenty of paper and pencils, it's quite easy to track.

Clem, the shark swam back over to the tee and majestically turned into a semblance of a golfer. Garland struck the ball with authority 230 yards straight up the middle. Chip followed with a similar shot of about 260 yards. Randall seemed to have difficulty figuring out what end of the club to hold. He swung hard and shanked the ball 25 yards out of bounds. He nearly cried until Garland finally granted him his one and only mulligan, which he chili-dipped into the left OB. He glared at Clem and then threw his club over at our golf cart.

I took another look at the course layout and decided to go for broke. The driver shaft was a bit whippier than I would have liked, so I would have to adjust for it. Instead of playing the shot up the middle of the fairway, I played a strong draw, almost hooking it off the fairway, cutting off the dogleg as best as I could.

Garland exploded in laughter that was immediately echoed by all of the golf staff. "Well, Sam, you're either very foolish, or that's the best hit I have ever seen on this hole."

When I played on the golf team at SDSU, the same team that led the NCAA for several years in a row, and won the national championship twice, I was told the same thing by the USC golf coach, right before we won the NCAA Golf Championship in Las Vegas that year.

We eventually found my ball a few yards off the front of the green. The drive was nearly 300 yards. It was a relatively easy chip and a putt for my first birdie of the day.

Unfortunately, I beat my new buddies Clem and Chip, on their own home course. I let them stop on the way back to the office so that they could get some cash from the bank so they could pay off their foolish bets. Poor Randall never recovered after the first hole and seemed to pick up his ball on most of the remaining holes. He somehow felt that he had let Clem down by not discovering that I was a scratch player. He felt responsible for not warning him ahead of time.

To make matters worse, when we went back to the office, everyone wanted to know who won. When Garland continued to ignore the questions, the office went silent. One of the junior managers didn't take the hint. He told me he was in charge of the employee golf team and would sure like to know what happened out there. I pulled a roll of cash out of my pocket and told him I got lucky and that I would love to put $100 in the company coffers towards the next team party event.

As Clem glared at me, somehow, I could just feel the love leaving our relationship.

10

Morals Clause – Mississippi style

The next day we flew back to San Diego. While I worked on my iPad, Randall drank until he fell asleep.

The next summons from Mississippi came the following week. Garland called and requested that I come back to town for a three-day series of workshops concerning the final integration of Leisure Pathways Technologies into SI. A couple of hours after the first phone call, he called back again. Would I please bring along our PR gal so that they could tie in our artwork and advertising campaigns with SI and its subsidiaries?

He didn't ask me to bring my golf clubs---and bringing my bowling ball might be pushing it.

I called our in-house travel department to arrange our flights and accommodations. A few minutes later, they called back and indicated that there were no rooms available in town. This was strange. Garland owned the only hotel in the area, and it always had vacancies. I gave him a callback, and he told me not to worry about it, he would take care of us both when we got into town. I could tell by the tone of his voice that he was trying to act civil, even though he probably now hated my guts.

I called Randall, but strangely, I could not find him. I usually just had to turn around and trip over him. I assumed he would want to tag along with us back to Mississippi. I also concluded that if Clem wanted him there, he could contact him, himself.

Sharon Holt, our VP of advertising, and I arrived in Mobile, Alabama, the following afternoon. The trip from Mobile to our destination was an adventure. A massive storm was hitting the area, leaving several inches of rain, causing nearly zero visibility. After renting a car, we drove off into the deluge. After several hours of dodging puddles, we arrived in Gautier. It was extremely dark and raining heavily. The little town had seemingly rolled up its sidewalks.

I called Garland on his cell phone, and he gave us directions to meet him out at the Country Club, the same place we had played our first *and probably* last round of golf.

The clubhouse had been closed for most of the day because of the heavy rain and flooding. There was a single light glowing in the lobby area.

As I parked the car, Sharon jumped out and said she would get our keys from Clem and be right back. More than ten minutes passed. Finally, Sharon and

Garland exited the building. He turned off the remaining light and securely locked the door. He waved to me as he hurried to his car to get out of the pouring rain, and then drove off.

"I hope he gave you good instructions on where our rooms are," I said as she entered the car. It took her a few moments to get settled into the front seat and shake off whatever water she could. It was so dark I could hardly see my hands in front of my face.

"He's not a very nice man," she said quietly. "He talked filthily and blew cigarette smoke in my face the entire time." Sharon was an attractive married woman in her mid-twenties. She had been with our company from almost the beginning.

"Yeah, he's a real piece of work," I replied, taking the large envelope from her and turning on the interior car lights. I shook the contents out on the seat. There was a plot map of the development with a big X marked on one of the units---and there was a single key---nothing else.

"Why only one key?" I asked.

"Beats me," she replied. "He was talking fast and was very suggestive. I never even saw what was in the envelope. I was just anxious to get out of there."

"Man, I smell a rat."

"What do you mean?"

"Well---they own the only hotel in town, that's conveniently fully booked---probably for the first time in history. And, they own several hundred units, just in this resort. Why only one key?"

I pulled out my cell phone and quickly dialed Clem.

"I'm sorry the party you are calling is not available at this time. Please try your call again later. Message 3901"

After three more attempts at calling him, I gave up and drove over to the X marked on the map.

It turned out to be better than I thought. It was a large, four-bedroom resort home, right on the golf course. All of the lights were turned on. There was a gift basket full of wine and fruit on the front table, including a little welcoming note from Garland. Hmm. Maybe I was wrong. After my last visit, I had assumed that I was a marked man with him.

We jumped back in the car and drove back into town and had a quick dinner at a seafood place. By the time we returned to the resort home, the rain had stopped, and we settled in for the night.

Sharon slept in the upstairs master bedroom, and I slept downstairs in one of the guestrooms. We left the food and wine untouched in its basket and turned in for the night. I was probably being overly sensitive after my last visit to Mississippi.

The next day in Garland's office, I found Randall sitting at the conference table having his morning drink, which appeared to be a Bloody Mary. He said that he had arrived late the previous evening. He acted somewhat nervous and maybe even a little fidgety. I didn't ask him where he had spent the night.

Sharon worked the next couple of days with a woman named Kathy Albright, who was SI's VP of Marketing in Houston.

I visited with several different executives from Southern's sales and marketing division. I kept on thinking I was being featured in an episode of *Mad Men*. These people ran their local office as if it was in the 60's or 1970s. All of the executives had liquor bottles stacked behind their desks. They only drank when the lights were on or when a dog barked anywhere in Mississippi, or if it was hot or cold outside. They would shoot the bull with each other until noon, and then they would drink a two-hour lunch, after which they would reluctantly return to the office for more drinks before departing early for the local saloon. No wonder Randall drank all of his meals.

Women executives seemed to be in short supply in Mississippi. The women were kept on a short leash and expected to make coffee and take detailed notes when the males were too lazy to do so themselves, which was all of the time. Kathy Albright and Sharon were hardly tolerated by this chauvinistic group.

71

Three days later, we all returned to California. Sharon and I sat together in first class, with Randall seated in the row directly behind us. As usual, after he had consumed his first few drinks, his light went off, and he slept the rest of the trip home.

11

● ● ● ● ● ● ● ● ● ● ● ● ● ● ● ●

Encinitas – Breakfast with Randall

On Sunday night, of that same week, Randall called me at home and asked me to join him for breakfast the following morning.

When I arrived at the Pancake House restaurant in Encinitas, he was already seated and was pretending to study a file folder on the table.

"Good morning, Randall," I said as I slipped into my seat across from him. "How's tricks?"

He looked uncomfortable for a moment before responding. "Sam," he said, as he looked down at his paperwork and slowly shook his head. "I'm afraid we're going to have to let you go. I'm really, very sorry."

I looked at him for a few seconds waiting for him to smile or laugh. He did neither.

"I assume you're kidding Randall," I replied calmly. "I have increased our bottom line, what 500%, a 1000%? That's not good enough for SI? You know, and I know that I have an employment contract. You can't fire me without cause. I run the most profitable division in SI. If you are serious---I'll sue your asses off!"

Randall's face was a picture of diplomacy. "You might want to think about that before you do anything that stupid," he replied.

"And, what's that supposed to mean?

Randall's somber look changed into a smirk. "Anyone who has any sense of business acumen---knows that you don't dip your pen in the company inkwell."

"Say it in English, Randall. I'm not screwing anyone. Names and dates---let's have them."

"It was stupid of you to sleep with your employee in front us during your Mississippi visit. Yeah, that was pretty ballsy of you to shack up together. I'm sure you understand that violates the 'morals clause' in your employment contract."

I suddenly realized that he wasn't kidding. I could feel my entire body begin to flush with anger. "You can do better than that, can't you? You're the ones who arranged the sleeping accommodations."

"Well, the videotape of you two is really quite explicit," he said, sadly shaking his head.

"You dumb shit," I said. "Why don't you show me a copy of your tapes? Or, better yet, send them to the newspapers? Do you think the travel industry would be interested? How about my wife? Are you going to share the grim evidence with her? Have your attorneys reviewed the tapes? It should be good for a laugh or two. I know nothing happened there. If there is a tape, it would be rated G---bring it on. Can you look at me straight in the eyes and tell me you have seen this tape, yourself?"

"No, but Clem said it was very graphic."

Now it was my turn to shake my head. "Let me guess. Garland is behind this whole deal, right? When Blackwell hears about this, he's going to be upset, and he's going to come down hard on both of you clowns."

"No!" said a flustered Randall. "This is coming down straight from the very top. Sure, Clem has a lot to do with the Sharon thing, and he'll be the one to take over your company, but this is coming from the top."

He rearranged his papers and removed one piece, and placed it to the side. "They also found out what your real numbers are. You aren't even profitable. You're barely keeping your company afloat." He tapped his index finger on the paper. "Figures don't lie---you know that."

"Randall, do you think for a moment that I would turn over my accounting to you guys? Sure, you sweep our accounts every night and deposit our funds in your master accounts to earn additional interest, but do you think I would be stupid enough, with millions of dollars at stake, to rely on your bookkeeping? You guys must be dumber than you look. I've got an audit trail on you a mile long. I've had my own CPA firm recording every document since you took over my company. The quarterly reports that you send me from corporate are gibberish. As you well know, they are unreadable. You don't think I know that you guys are shifting my profits to other divisions so that you don't have to pay me my earn-out? Guess again, Randall."

Randall stood up as he put his papers back in their folder. He looked sad for a moment, and then his look changed to that of just plain mean. "You don't know who you're fucking with, Sam. They eat people like you for breakfast. That's a quote from Blackwell himself. It doesn't matter if this stuff is true or not. If you try to sue them about this matter, they will make your life hell on earth. This is the big leagues, whether you like it or not. You made a few million, now move on to something else, before you get hurt."

I also stood and grabbed Randall's arm near his bicep. "Just a minute, Randall. That almost sounded like a threat. Are you saying that if I cause any problems, you're going to try and harm me in some fashion?"

Without hesitation, Randall tried to pull his arm away from me. I let it go, and he stumbled up against the wall.

"You've got to grow up quick if you want to get out of this thing in one piece, Sam. They paid you good money for your company. Take it and run. You were lucky. You hit a home run. Now move on.

They never figured you would even have a chance at making such a large earn-out. Nobody increases earnings by 1000%. No one even considered you could do that. Just because they wear three-piece business suits and live in big mansions and are quoted in Forbes from time to time doesn't mean they play by the rules---just the opposite, in fact. If they can keep $20 or $30 million from being paid in earn-outs and bring the money down to the bottom line in another subsidiary---they'll do it. They'll do it every time."

He turned and started to leave the restaurant.

Before he could complete his turn, I took hold of his arm again until he fully stopped. "Tell your friends at SI that I got their message. Tell them for me, that I look forward to seeing them in court. I met some guys in Iraq that thought they were pretty tough too. I'm still here---they aren't. Tell SI they better think twice before they try to make this anything more than a court case."

He jerked his arm free again and stumbled towards the door. "You have a restraining order issued against you. You have an hour to pack up your personal things and move out of the offices. If you're there after an hour, we will have you arrested. Enjoy the rest of your day. Oh, by the way, don't forget to pick up Mikey on the way home from work. If kids aren't picked up on time by their parents, someone else might have to do it for them."

He ran out the door before I could wring his neck.

12

• • • • • • • • • • • • • • •

Escondido – Come on everybody it's poly time!

I went back to my office and was greeted out front by two bored-looking sheriff deputies. They escorted me into my office and waited while I packed my personal belongings.

By this time, I had leased almost every building in our office park. Hundreds of employees were usually moving back and forth between offices. Today there was no one outside, but I could see several people peeking out of their windows, quietly watching the show outside, probably wondering what the hell was going on.

The deputies followed me to my car. "By the way," I said, "do either of you know who does the polygraph work for your office?"

They both shook their heads, but one of them gave me a card with the headquarters information on it.

I dialed the number as I drove off the parking lot of Leisure Pathway Technologies for the last time.

I was transferred twice before I eventually talked with someone who had some answers. "For all of our polygraph work, we use a retired sheriff's deputy, Ralph Landers, who's gone into private practice. He runs a small security company over in Escondido. There's no one better."

Two hours later, I was about to be wired up to a polygraph machine, in Lander's office. Ralph Landers was a quiet man, and I could tell he took his job very seriously. He must have entered law enforcement in his early twenties, and retired after an additional twenty. He was still a young man.

I could feel my heart rate race as he attached the first few sensors. He had asked me to prepare a list of questions for him to ask me. He studied my notes, made a few notations then began asking me a series of mundane questions---to help settle my nerves and to calibrate my answers. Landers then asked me the following questions:

"Have you ever had sexual intercourse with Sharon Holt?"

Answer: "No."

"Have you had any kind of relationship with Sharon Holt other than strictly business?"

Answer: "No."

"Are you using a CPA firm to record all of your business transactions at Leisure PT?"

Answer: "Yes."

"Was this CPA firm hired by you without the knowledge of Southern Industries?"

"**Answer**: "Yes."

"To your knowledge, have profits for Leisure PT increased substantially since its acquisition by SI?"

Answer: "Yes."

"To your knowledge, has Southern been involved in any possible fraudulent transactions with the Leisure PT?"

Answer: "Yes."

"Are the fraudulent transactions in regards to their accounting procedures?"

Answer: "Yes."

"Has anyone representing Southern Industries ever threatened your well-being or the well-being of your family?"

Answer: "Yes."

I passed the test with flying colors. I was now ready to begin my pursuit of SI.

The following day I sent a cover letter and a certified copy of the polygraph test directly to Jack Blackwell at SI's headquarters in Houston. I let two days pass and then gave him a call at his office. He refused to take my call.

I got on the Internet and looked up the database for attorneys in San Diego. With a couple of clicks, I found what I was looking for---a list of the recipients for the Attorney of the Year Award from the American Bar Association.

The following day I had meetings with the top three attorneys from the ABA list. I gave them a copy of my daily journal, which indicated the entire history of Leisure Pathway Technologies, from the acquisition through the threats in the restaurant. I also included a copy of the polygraph test.

The next morning, when I checked my voicemail, I had several messages with eight of them coming from one of the attorneys, Benjamin Kiddrick. Kiddrick had been the most recent recipient of the ABA award and was well known for successfully taking on big companies and city governments.

I was learning one of my first lessons involving lawsuits. The best attorneys will represent you if the opposing party is big and has deep pockets. My attorney would win financially regardless of who won the lawsuit.

"I want to represent you," Kiddrick stated emphatically. "It will be a long fight but if we can catch a few breaks and get these guys in front of a jury, we'll kill them.

That evening Jenny and I went out to eat at Jakes restaurant in Del Mar and sat at a table looking out over the beach. It was low tide, and we watched quietly as the waves became calmer and the sun made its last appearance of the day.

I had filled her in on the recent activities from SI. I told her about our new attorney and his reputation. She seemed pleased to hear about this initial progress.

"Are you going to be okay with the lawsuit thing," I asked. "It could be hectic for quite some time. We are in the right. I'm confident that everything will work out for us, okay."

Jenny took a sip of her drink and closed her eyes for a moment. When she opened them, they were sparkling with confidence. "I know we will be okay. At any other time, I would be concerned. This time though, I know we are in the right, and we have the best law firm possible to represent us. We also have a full bank account. Best of all, you can stop all of the travel now and be home for a while. Your family has missed you.

13

● ● ● ● ● ● ● ● ● ● ● ● ● ● ●

San Clemente – Who's crazy?

I was advised by Kiddrick to stop looking for new employment and instead start meeting with a psychologist on at least a weekly basis. This would be an indication to the court if I won, that I was suffering from severe mental trauma, and it might be worth more compensation when the trial was finally over.

I have never been involved in a lawsuit before. On television, a lawsuit lasts almost sixty minutes. In real life, it lasts quite a bit longer, how much longer I was about to find out. It could be exceptionally long if you are fighting a Fortune 500 company. With their kind of money, they could make almost any problem go away or delay it forever.

Within a week after filing my lawsuit against SI, Kiddrick received a phone call from one of the largest law firms in San Diego, announcing that they had been retained to handle the lawsuit for Southern. A few days later, another major law firm contacted him and said they had also been retained to represent Clem Garland and Western Resorts International. They promised Kiddrick that they would start manufacturing enough complaints, countersuits, and discovery nonsense to keep him and his firm busy for years while they prepared for trial.

Years? Are you kidding me? Years? And, Kiddrick wanted me to do nothing until we finally ended up in court.

My first meeting with my new shrink was coming up tomorrow. Maybe he could give me some good advice about being complacent for the next few years while I waited for my case to reach trial.

I didn't expect that to work out.

My drive north to San Clemente was uneventful. In the bright red turbo Porsche, it was a source of pure enjoyment.

---Boys and their toys.

It was not exactly a low-profile ride. With the radar detector cranked up high, I wasn't too concerned about the attention of the Highway Patrol. The highway between Oceanside and San Clemente is known for its wide-open speeds. With only the Pacific Ocean on the west side of Interstate 5 and Camp Pendleton on the east side, even VWs traveled at 80 MPH. While some passengers in nearby cars gave me a thumb's up as I passed them, others saluted me, good-naturedly with their middle finger. Love Southern California.

A motorcyclist had been following me since Encinitas. He was nearly a mile back, and I probably would not have even noticed him if he hadn't acted abnormally when the traffic started backing up as I neared the Inspection Station just south of San Clemente. Motorcyclists generally used this congestion opportunity to dodge through the different lanes of traffic, passing hundreds of cars in the process. I watched as the motorcyclist stayed behind a white van and made no attempt to save time and beat the traffic.

Was it a coincidence that he followed me all the way to the turnoff for the shrink's office? Was it Freud who said, "There are no coincidences in life?"

Feeling like I was starring in a B rated detective movie, I started watching my rearview mirror with increased awareness.

With minimal difficulty, I found the office of the shrink, just off the main drag in Downtown San Clemente.

The doctor's actual office was an adjunct to his home and looked like a quaint Mexican casita with a side entry. Elevator music was playing softly in the background as I entered a small reception area. A hand-printed sign on the coffee table said that the doctor would be with me shortly and to take a seat, be quiet, and turn off any cell phone devices.

My type-A personality disorder kicked in after about a 15 minutes wait. I rechecked my watch and was ready to leave when the door opened, and Dr. Zable made his entrance.

He was tall and thin with a dramatic goatee, which was colored a fierce coal black with two snow-white streaks leading away from his chin. It perfectly matched his slicked-back hair. A lot of coordination had gone on between the good doctor and his cosmetologist.

Dr. Erwin Zable, Ph.D., was a piece of work.

Before saying a word, he checked his iPad and scrolled down the screen a couple of times before looking up.

"Samuel? Are you Samuel Barns?"

Who else would I be? "Yes---that would be me."

He nodded his head with a serious look on his face. With measured steps, he walked away from me and placed his iPad on a nearby desk, squared it exactly parallel to the edge. and then returned to stand in front of me. "Dr. Erwin Zable," he said and stuck out his hand.

I stood and then shook it. He held on to it longer than was needed and then reluctantly let it go.

"Let's try that handshake again," he said.

I shook his hand again, trying hard not to roll my eyes in disbelief. He kept squeezing harder and harder, for whatever reason, until I squeezed him hard to the point of making his face turn red.

"That's better, Samuel. Is it alright if I call you Samuel?"

"Just Sam would be fine."

He took my elbow and guided me over to a comfortable chair and motioned for me to sit. He retrieved his iPad and placed it on his lap as he sat down across from me.

"I can tell you that you have been damaged. I had a brief conversation with your attorney the other day, and he voiced his concerns."

Okay, I'll bite. "What was your first clue that I was damaged?"

"The way you shook hands. It lacked confidence and strength. I want you to practice shaking hands with other people before our next meeting."

I didn't think that it was a question, so I just sat and waited for him to continue.

"While we are discussing our next meeting, I want you to do something for me." He paused, waiting for me to ask him what?

I waited.

"What did you dream about last night, Sam?"

"I don't recall."

"Do you think it was a pleasant dream or a nightmare?"

"As I said, I don't recall."

He typed briefly on the iPad.

"It might be too traumatic for you to remember. What do you think?"

"As I said earlier, I don't recall any of my dreams from last night."

"Hmm." He paused for a moment, deep in thought. "Alright, here is what I want you to do. Get a sharp pencil and a notepad and place it next to your bed. Whenever you have a dream, I want you to wake up and write it down so that we can discuss it during your next visit. By discussing your dreams, we will know what is going on in your subconscious. It is important to remember that *dreams are the window to your soul.*"

"I thought that the *eyes were the window to your soul.*"

"Whatever---just make sure to keep track of all of your dreams. Now I want you to lean back in your chair and get as comfortable as you can and close your eyes and relax. I'm going to help you get into a very relaxed state. I am then going to ask you some questions, nothing tricky---and I want you to respond without contemplating your answer. There are no right or wrong answers."

He spent the next couple of minutes trying to relax me by soothingly mentioning that my legs and arms were so relaxed that they were falling asleep. My breathing was slowing as I relaxed my body, etc.

"Sam, what was the name of your last company?"

"Leisure Pathway Technologies. Everyone referred to it as Leisure PT."

"What was your position with this company?"

"I was the president, CEO, and Founder."

"Why were you fired?"

"Because the assholes didn't want to pay me according to our agreed upon contract."

"Wasn't the real reason you left---because they caught you having an affair with one of your employees?"

"That's what they claimed---but it didn't happen. They wanted to keep the money that they owed me."

"Do you have any guns at home?"

"Yes. I have one gun."

"Have you considered using it on yourself, because of this current traumatic conflict?"

"No, that would be difficult. It is a 22-caliber target rifle that I competed with in college."

"Have you thought about hurting yourself?"

"Not myself. The folks at Southern---oh yeah."

The questions continued on in this manner for some time, and I noticed that he was slowing down and getting almost repetitive.

I cracked my eyes a little and noticed that he was lying back in his chair with his own eyes directed towards the ceiling while he judiciously picked his nose, examined the results, and then flicked them to the side onto the carpet.

Three more years of this? Not a chance.

14

Rancho Santa Fe – Real Estate

A few days later, I canceled my next appointment with Dr. Z and told him I would call him when we got closer to a trial date. He took the news well and hardly whimpered before he reluctantly hung up his phone. He was going to miss my $300 per hour nose-picking sessions.

My next call was to an old marine buddy of mine, Mickey Riley. We had spent quite a bit of time together during the Gulf war. After we rotated back to the states, he came to visit me in San Diego and had decided to stay.

I was selling real estate at a small subdivision near Rancho Penasquitos. I talked him into getting his real estate license, and he took over my position when I left to start a mortgage company, one of my first attempts at becoming an entrepreneur.

Mickey had spent a couple of years in sales and then had moved to the construction side of the business. The last time we had talked, he was just completing a small subdivision in the area.

We decided to meet for lunch at a comfortable little restaurant in downtown Rancho Santa Fe called Quimby's. As usual, the place was crowded and noisy.

Rancho Santa Fe is an iconic moneyed town often cited as the priciest zip code in the nation. 80% of the shop space, in the small commercial center of the village, consisted of real estate offices and stock brokerage firms. The agents and brokers from these firms ensured that Quimby's was crowded every day. There was also the usual sprinkling of much older men with much younger, hot wives, often with two or three small children and a nanny. Yes, even their nanny.

I spotted Mickey in a corner booth and worked my way over to him and took a seat. I looked over at my old friend as we scrutinized the menu. He looked as tough as any marine I had ever known and still kept himself in top physical condition.

We talked about old times and my current problems with Southern while we waited for our food. We both ordered the same thing, two large Cobb salads. We had considered the huge gourmet burgers, but times have changed, and we were trying to change too.

I told him about the threats from SI and that I had been having people following me lately. He needlessly suggested that I should be taking extra precautions in case they became more serious, and I conceded that I had recently come to the same conclusion.

Finally, I got to the real purpose of our lunch together. I told him I was dying of boredom and needed to get back into some type of work. I explained that the law firm had suggested that I not work at all and spend my free time with their appointed shrink, but that just wasn't working out. If I didn't get active with something soon, I would consider harming myself. He might have understood I was kidding.

He thought for a moment and then said that he had just started a new fun project that was bigger than anything he had done in the past. He said he needed to make a few phone calls before he could promise me anything.

Mickey promised to give me a call the following day.

As we left the restaurant, I noticed a motorcyclist parked in the shade across the street from the restaurant. He dropped down his visor and started his engine as I got into my car.

15

• • • • • • • • • • • • • • • •

Working in Fairbanks Ranch

The following week I started my new job as the VP of Sales and Marketing for a major housing developer headquartered out of Santa Monica, California, near LA.

They owned several large projects in San Diego, including a new master-planned subdivision for luxury homes called Fairbanks Ranch, in Rancho Santa Fe. They needed new management to kick it into gear and turn it into a reality.

Mickey had also recently been hired as the VP of construction for the Fairbanks community. We would be working together, at least at that project daily.

I was responsible for several projects in Southern California. We had a new luxury community that was being built on a beautiful piece of land on the Coronado bayfront.

To the north, I often had to visit our corporate offices in Santa Monica, as well as several projects north of Los Angeles.

While I thought I had been busy at SI, this new real estate job was extremely time-consuming. I would arrive early in the morning at my local office in Fairbanks Ranch Plaza, and often not leave there until midnight.

I'll admit, I could have slacked off more and cut back on my hours and duties, and still gone an adequate job, but with the future litigation I was facing with SI, I knew I was going to be under the microscope.

SI had filed several charges against me. Not only was the violation of the 'morals clause' of my employment contract under fire, but there were also claims of incompetence and cooked books.

The last thing I needed was to do poorly at my new job. SI would be the first ones to point out the incompetence and bring to the attention of the court.

I needed to demonstrate to everyone that I was a hard worker and a successful manager. I was being paid more money now than I had been earning at SI. I needed to show people I was worth it.

~ ~***~ ~

"Mr. Barker...this is Friedman. He has been hired to manage several housing projects in San Diego. This should tie him up for a while. Do you want me to introduce myself and make his life more interesting?" He listened

to the response from the man on the other end. *"I fully understand, sir. I've got it covered."*

The man restarted his motorcycle and raced off down San Dieguito Road towards Santaluz.

16

• • • • • • • • • • • • • •

A little Fairbanks Ranch history

Fairbanks Ranch is a hidden jewel located about seven miles inland from the Del Mar Race Track---*Where the Surf meets the Turf in Old Del Mar.*

When the racetrack first opened in 1939, it became the favorite getaway place for the rich and famous from Hollywood.

The San Dieguito River snakes its way from San Pasqual to the east, through Escondido, into Rancho Santa Fe, and it eventually empties into the Pacific Ocean just to the west side of the race track.

The river basin is surrounded by some of the most pristine acreages in all of Southern California---even though it was a pokelogan maze in several areas.

From its inception, the patrons of the racetrack soon realized that this was not just a place to gamble and party. It was a place to invest and even live, to escape the rigors of the movie industries. Stars like Pat O'Brien, Bing Crosby, Gary Cooper, Oliver Hardy, Danny Kaye, Gene Kelly, Mary Pickford, and Douglas Fairbanks frequented the area on a regularly. Several of the stars purchased large tracks of land within the valley for their own residences and investments.

Fairbanks Ranch was the former estate of Douglas Fairbanks and his wife Mary Pickford and is considered one of the preeminent locations in the entire nation. It is situated over nearly five square miles of beautiful rolling hills with views of the Pacific Ocean to the west and the Cuyamaca Mountains to the east.

The plan was to develop this massive piece of property into a world-class residential estate community. It would offer its future owners extensive equestrian facilities and trails, a country club, golf course, tennis courts and spacious residential estate lots to be built out to an owner's personal specifications.

Mickey and I had our jobs cut out for us. All we had to do was implement a marketing plan that would attract multi-millionaires from around the world. Then convince them to purchase land that consisted primarily of rolling hills, several groves of orange and avocado trees, thousands of rattlesnakes, no infrastructure (roads or utilities), and build it out as quickly as possible.

~ ~***~ ~

During my first week on the job, Mickey and I spent most of our time trying to familiarize ourselves with the project. It was exhaustive work. Even though San Diego is usually well known for its temperate climate, during August, it could get sizzling hot.

Wearing jeans, T-shirts, and boots, we tried to inspect large sections of the project each day, taking copious notes on how each lot should be graded out for its highest and best use. We hardly looked like executives as we trudged over the raw land, which was covered in brush, taking frequent water breaks whenever possible. It was almost worse than our memories of boot camp.

On the second day, Mickey found an error in the placement of one of the grading stake locations. He made a few notations on his plot map and moved forward a few feet to see if he could locate the boundary line monument.

"Mickey, freeze, don't move even the slightest bit. Rattlesnake on your right---I've got it."

I moved in on the snake as it coiled itself, and started to rattle like a pair of castanets. I approached it from behind and drove a shovel at it, severing its head. Even without its head, the body remained coiled, and the rattles continued to make their eerie noise. The deadly jaws of the snake constricted back forth several times before it finally stopped moving.

I looked over at what was left of the snake and shook my head. "Those things freak me out. I've almost stepped on them a dozen times, and I've even had a few strike at me and miss. They blend in with their surroundings. I've seen some in grassy areas like this, and they are almost the same color green as the shrubs, while others are the color of dirt when they are lying beside a road or pathway."

I looked over at Mickey and saw that he was deep in thought about something. I dug a quick hole and buried the snake and its head as deep as possible.

"You know what's the worst thing about a snakebite?" he asked rhetorically. "The bill from the hospital. A friend of mine has a kid who got bit by a rattlesnake in the parking lot over at UCSD. His bill was $143,000. Seriously! The antivenin that they use is more valuable than gold. If the snake doesn't kill you, the bill will."

He looked over at me and grinned. "By the way, thanks for the heads up."

"No problem. It reminds me of that famous snake story involving Davy Crockett."

"What snake story?"

"The one where Davy and his Indian scout were tracking deer way out in the wilderness. They shot this big old buck, and while skinning it, their horses ran off in all the confusion. On the second day, their horses still hadn't returned, so they decided they better try and hike back to civilization. The Indian headed over towards some bushes to take a quick leak when all of a sudden, he screamed and rushed back over to Davy.

"The Indian explained that he had been bitten by the biggest, meanest rattler that he had ever seen. Davy asked him where he was bitten. He raised up his small loincloth and pointed. He had been bitten right at the end of his penis. It was up to Davy to save his friend. He helped him find a nice shady tree, gathered some water and venison, and took off running towards the closest settlement in hopes of finding a doctor.

"A day and a half later, Davy found the settlement, and fortunately they had a doctor. Davy asked him what to do about a snake bite. "Well first you make a few cuts around the bite marks, then you put your mouth over the wound and suck like crazy. Make sure you get as much of the poison out as you can, without swallowing any, then wrap the area up as best as possible and get your friend back here as soon as possible. If you don't do this exactly how I've directed, your friend could die."

Davy Crockett borrowed a horse and slowly rode back to the big tree where his friend lay moaning in pain. By now his penis was as big as his arm and an angry purple color.

"What did the doctor say, Davy?" asked the Indian as he grimaced with pain.

Davy took off his raccoon hat and solemnly placed it over his heart before he spoke. "He said you're going to die, Injun."

17

· · · · · · · · · · · · · ·

Playing with the big boys

Within a week after filing my initial lawsuit, a white service van was discovered parked by the curb, a hundred or so yards down the street from my home.

We had started our neighborhood watch program the previous year. To my knowledge, nothing had been reported unusual since its inception until one of my neighbors noticed the suspicious-looking vehicle parked in the neighborhood for several days in multiple locations. He first called Jenny and asked her if she had noticed the van, and she replied that she had not. His second call was to the sheriff's department. Fifteen minutes later, two County Sheriff vehicles surrounded the van.

Three former FBI agents and a private investigator were seated in the back of the van that seemed to have enough electrical equipment to track a satellite into orbit and back again. They had installed listening devices on all of my phones. They were also using some type of advanced laser technology to monitor and record our conversations by reading the vibrations off of the glass windows in our home. They refused to disclose who had hired them. They were arrested for trespassing and a few other charges. As soon as they posted their bail, they disappeared on the next flight leaving San Diego, never to be seen again.

The giant Southern was flexing its financial muscle. They used every possible ploy to delay every process required under the lawsuit.

If a complaint requested a fifteen-day deadline, their high-priced legal beagles would wait until the fifteenth day to request a ninety-day delay for any number of reasons. With two major law firms being tasked with using any delay tactics imaginable, and an open checkbook, there seemingly was no end in sight from the never-ending mountains of correspondence and discovery requests. Of course, my legal bills continued to run 7/24.

A couple of weeks later, Jenny called me at the office and told me to get to Mikey's school as soon as possible. It was an emergency. She would meet me there.

Mikey was going to a private school in Rancho Santa Fe, only a few minutes from my office.

Jenny was pulling into the school parking lot at just about the same time I arrived. There were three sheriff's cars parked in front of the administration office with their emergency lights flashing. A terrible sense of dread spread over me as I raced into the building.

Jenny and I saw the officers speaking attentively with the school administrators. Just beyond them, I saw Mikey sitting in a chair next to the school nurse. I ran over to him, and he jumped up and hugged me. He immediately started crying and then realized he was ten years old and attempted to stop the tears.

"Dad! A guy tried to grab me. He wanted me to go with him. I remembered what you said---and took off running as fast as I could. I screamed for Mr. Donnelly, and he chased the man into the parking lot."

By now, Jenny was holding him too. She was making soft, calming sounds as Mikey continued to try and hold back the tears.

I walked over to one of the deputies and introduced myself. He motioned to his partner, and they requested that I go into another room with them. I waived to Jenny and pointed where I was going and then left with them.

A deputy with a nametag reading *Sgt. Busby* motioned me towards a seat and took one himself across from me.

"At approximately 1:45 p.m. this afternoon, a male suspect entered the school grounds and approached your son during recess. He told your son that you had asked him to pick up him up and bring him over to the golf course. When Mikey said that he wasn't allowed to go anywhere with strangers, the man told him he would pick him up and carry him to the car if need be. At that point, Mikey took off running for the principal's office, screaming all of the way there. The principal---Mr. Donnelly was just leaving his office when he heard the commotion and chased after the suspect. He was able to get a good, partial plate number before the guy took off. We checked it out and found that a car with that plate was stolen earlier this morning." He checked his notes further and turned several more pages on his notepad before continuing. "I think that is about it. Can you think of anyone who might want to kidnap your son? Anyone at all?"

"Yes, I know exactly who did it. Proving it though might be entirely different, though," I said.

"What's the man's name?" asked the deputy, showing some enthusiasm.

"I don't know his name, but I know the name of the company he works for," I said. I then proceeded to tell him my tales of woe about Southern Industries. When I completed my story, after several minutes, I looked at both of the deputies for some type of reaction.

Busby looked at his partner before speaking. "Quite frankly, it probably was someone hired by Southern. Based on what you've told us, they could be trying to carry out some of their threats."

"So can you arrest someone, or is it going to be like the other times they've broken law?"

110

"I'm sorry, Mr. Barns, but until we have proof they are connected with this crime, I'm afraid we can't do much."

"Can you at least talk to them and inform them that they are being considered suspects?"

"Not really," said Busby.

"Can you pick up the guy that has been following me on his motorcycle for the past several months, and find out where he was today?"

"The suspect was driving a car, not a motorcycle."

"And, he couldn't steal a car and park his motorcycle while he was trying to kidnap my son?"

"I suppose that's possible."

"Could you at least pull him over, take a couple of pictures of him and see if Mikey or the principal can recognize him?"

They agreed that they would contact the motorcyclist if they could find him.

They looked for him during the following week, with no success, and then gave up. Two weeks later, he was back to following me again.

In the meantime, Jenny could no longer hide her fears about our family getting hurt. She started avoiding going into her real estate office. She would drive Mikey to school and often spend half the day sitting in their parking lot, watching out for Southern kidnappers. She was turning into a nervous wreck.

Jenny and I needed to discuss these latest events.

"I thought that this would be a normal lawsuit if there is such a thing. What I didn't consider was that you and Mikey might be at risk. This changes everything. Maybe we should re-think this entire situation."

Jenny hugged me, then stepped back. "What do you have in mind?"

"I'm making good money now, better than I was making at SI. I'm happy with my job. Maybe we should consider dropping the lawsuit. Maybe we should move on."

I could see the color return to her face before she even answered. "We're not going to let those bastards win. Those thugs have threatened our family and our livelihood. We just need to regroup and go on the offense instead of reacting to all of their threats and bullshit."

I've been married to Jenny for more than ten years. In that entire time, I could count on one hand, she has sworn out loud, and still have several fingers remaining. Jenny was pissed. Nobody screwed with her family.

I re-contacted the polygraph operator, Ralph Landers, and set up a meeting with him. I brought him up to date on the kidnapping attempt of Mikey.

"You probably have two choices, Sam. You can keep him out of school for a while, just let him stay at home, where he can be easily protected, or I will go over to the school and work with their administrators on making their school a safer environment. I've given lectures to schools several times about how to keep their children safe. Very few children are ever kidnapped from schools. There are quite a few instances of predator events, though, taking place across the country. My speech informs the children what to do in case of an emergency. We have had rave reviews from the children, their parents, and the administration. I think that I would suggest the latter."

"Couldn't they just strong-arm the school and send a group of thugs in to kidnap him?" I asked.

"Of course, they could, but I would think it would be very unlikely. If they really wanted to kidnap your son, they could have just walked up to him and hit him over the head and carried him out of the school. Sam, they just want to remind you that they have control over your life. Nothing would make them happier than to have you withdraw your lawsuit after scaring you and your family half to death. I really think this was just another warning to you."

"Okay, Ralph, that makes sense, I suppose. Go with the lecture at the school, and let's monitor it for the time being. I also want you to entire someone to sit in the school parking lot while he is at school---just to be extra safe."

~ ~***~ ~

A month later, my beeper went off at 3:45 a.m. At first, I thought it was time to get up for my run, and I was halfway out of bed and into my running gear when it beeped again. It was a message from my superintendent at one of my large projects down on Coronado Island. I quickly called him back.

"Ted, what's going on?"

"Sam, turn on your television immediately."

"What channel?"

"Any of them. It should be on all channels by now. After you see it, we need you down here asap."

The Channel 10 helicopter was circling high above my Coronado project. Towering flames were reaching hundreds of feet into the air. The project consisted of four hundred luxury condominiums built right on the bayfront in Coronado. We were in advanced framing at the time, and I was watching a forest worth of framing being consumed in a ferocious blaze. Prices for the homes were expected to start in the low $2 millions. I was watching a billion-dollar fire.

Twenty minutes later, I was down at the construction site watching as fire crews diligently attempted to extinguish the remaining hot spots that kept reigniting throughout the project.

By mid-morning, I was surrounded by hundreds of police, firefighters, insurance adjusters, and reporters.

Being the company representative on-site, everyone was asking me questions.

I fielded questions for more than two hours. As I answered the questions, I was having a constant battle with myself as to who might have started the fire. Was it one of the construction companies, who had already made millions off the project, ensuring that they would rebuild and re-bill the project again? Was it a vendor who wanted to supply millions of dollars worth of building products again? Was it a competitor who wanted to set us back for a year while they brought their competing project to the market? Or, worse of all, was it Southern Industries trying to poison my position and longevity at my company? Without my income from my current job, would I be able to proceed with my multi-million-dollar lawsuit against them?

I worked these questions over and over again in my mind as my thoughts ran wild. If I told the arson investigators about my problems with Southern, would I lose my job even if Southern wasn't involved?

Quite frankly, I would fire me. It was a considerable chance for any company to take. If I were going to attract arson attacks on company projects, I would get as far away from me as possible.

In the end, I decided to pull the lead arson investigator aside and tell him about Southern. I couldn't live with myself if I didn't, and it was only fair to my company.

After an hour of discussion, he put away his notes, looked at his watch, and stood up. "It's a nice story, but I don't think a Fortune 500 Company would do something like this. I'll, of course, pass this info up the line, but I just don't see it."

At least I told them the truth, and the fact was, I wouldn't put anything past Southern.

Two months later, we were ready to start building again in Coronado. This time, it was a little bit different. I hired Ralph Landers and his company to design and implement a secure project, where there were now only ashes. With new fences and everyone working on the project being required to wear an ID badge, we were ready to get serious again.

It would be easier to steal NATO secrets from the nearby General Dynamics facility than to light a match at our project.

18

Out of the ashes

A year went by with very little advancement towards any settlement or relief from the flood of legal paperwork.

The law firms sent out various legal documents as part of their discovery process. It was mostly extensive interrogatories requesting additional answers to questions and further clarifications. Southern rarely answered their paperwork on time, and never answered them completely, requiring further time and effort to get the required information on the record.

In Kiddrick's legal offices, an entire room was designated as a depository for the prolific mass of redundant paperwork. They had threatened to bury us in paper, and they were fulfilling their promise.

~ ~***~ ~

That year, and the one following passed by rapidly. I will admit, though, that both had been two of the best years of my entire life.

We were able to build a substantial amount of the development in record time, and we were now selling the large estate lots to interested buyers.

The Fairbanks Ranch Country Club was up and running as well, and the Ted Robinson designed golf course was spectacular. On weekends I would often take Mikey over to the course and hit golf balls. At age twelve, he was developing into a good ball striker.

Life at home had settled down to a more manageable pace. Jenny and Mikey thought less about the lawsuit with each passing day. It was music to my ears to hear Jenny laugh out loud at times. Even though my hours were long and tenuous, I was at least at home in the evenings. We were functioning as a healthy family again.

It was not unusual for those of us in management to work 12 to 15-hour days to get the developments close to completion.

Our first sales release for the Fairbanks Ranch estate lots was a resounding success. Our sales force had done a magnificent job, and I was proud of them and our entire crew. For me, though, it was time for a small change.

I talked to the home office in Santa Monica, and within a couple of short weeks, I had hired my own replacement for VP of Sales and Marketing and became, instead, the managing broker for the sales operation. A demotion? It depends on how you looked at it. My salespeople were earning more than almost anyone in the company, if not the industry. All of them were driving (and affording) new Mercedes automobiles, and one even drove a bright red Rolls Royce. The least productive of the sales group was earning at least twice what I had been making as a VP.

Not only was I now supervising my small staff of agents, but I was also selling homes and estate lots myself. Within the first few months, I had earned more money than I had the entire previous year. Not only that, but I was also entertaining clients and potential clients while enjoying the daily perks of the Fairbanks Country Club and Golf Course. I was even back to being a scratch golfer again.

There is only one problem when life goes this well. Nothing good seems to last forever.

19

● ● ● ● ● ● ● ● ● ● ● ● ● ● ●

Southern turns up the heat

In Rancho Santa Fe, there is no mail delivery. The mail is delivered only to PO Boxes. Although new residents questioned this lack of home delivery, whenever it was brought to a vote, the residents always voted against mail delivery.

There are two fundamental beliefs regarding this decision. One is that many of the residents are wealthy, famous, or both, and they want their privacy. They don't want an unexpected surprise showing up on their front doorstep at inopportune times. The other reason is that the homes in Rancho Santa Fe are generally on large pieces of real estate. Many residents have never been to their neighbor's house, and it is usually hard for them to see each other when they are five or more acres apart and landscaped with hundreds of eucalyptus trees. Many of the residents love the opportunity of picking up their mail each day at the post office because it gives them the chance of actually seeing their neighbors and friends in their natural habitat. Even a multi-million-dollar mansion can get lonely without outside stimulus.

There are two main post offices in Rancho Santa Fe, the Town office, and the Del Rayo office near the entry to Fairbanks Ranch.

I pulled into the Del Rayo Shopping Plaza and parked my car in front of the Post Office. On my way in, I greeted two or three people before I got to my box. Because I have to pick up my mail almost every day, I treat it like I treat making my coffee in the morning. I am usually thinking about everything else other than getting my mail---and everything is kind of automatic. I turned the key in the lock and pulled out a stack of mail, two or three inches thick, most of it junk mail, which is typical for the residents of such a high-income area.

I moved over to one of the sorting tables and started sifting through the envelopes and tossing those of little or no interest. It was apparent, almost immediately, that something was different today. I usually received one letter from my attorney, each month---an invoice for copying fees used to respond to Southern and their delaying tactics.

Today there were three letters from Kiddrick and eight letters from the two law firms representing Southern and Clem Garland. A new firm was also in the stack. This was a new law firm that had been hired to coordinate between the two existing firms for Southern.

If they would just pay me what they were spending on their own lawyers, we wouldn't have to go to trial.

A quick phone call to Kiddrick confirmed the new attention from Southern. They had exhausted their extensions and was now being ordered to proceed with the final discovery aspect of the lawsuit. It was time for depositions. That was the good news---and the bad news.

According to the law, we could only subpoena, for deposition purposes, those persons who were in California. If they were not in California, we would have to go to them, wherever in the world they might be. Southern had closed our San Diego office shortly after firing me. Most of my former employees were now living in either Texas, Mississippi, or in any number of other states or countries where SI had regional offices.

It was going to cost me a small fortune to fund our trips across the country during the next 12 months. Hotels, airlines, court reporters, food, and associated travel costs were going to have to be paid out of my own pocket. This would be a massive undertaking and consume copious amounts of time and money.

Fortunately, the real estate boom had paid me handsomely. We had recently moved into a new home in Fairbanks so that I could be closer to work and family.

Maybe I could take on the behemoth, Southern.

It was time to start playing hardball.

20

· · · · · · · · · · · · · · ·

Guns and fun in Arizona

The following week I made two affirmative decisions. The first was to try and calm my family about sudden activities that were being generated by SI. Our family meeting went well, but I could also see that the protective shell that they had raised to protect themselves was struggling to be maintained. I decided it might be best to share only critical news with them as we proceeded towards trial.

My next affirmative action was to jump into my bright red Porsche and drive over to Scottsdale, Arizona.

As I traveled north up highway 15, I noticed a familiar motorcycle following me a mile or so back. It seemed as though I always saw motorcycles in my rearview mirror.

I passed through Temecula and then Riverside. I waited until I had reached Vandenberg Air Force base, and heavy traffic, before taking an off-ramp, on a curve of the highway. I parked under the overpass for a bit longer. Then I cut across some service streets to Morena Valley, rejoined the highway again, and proceeded to HWY 10 that would take me across the Mojave Desert and straight into to Phoenix---and on to Scottsdale.

As soon as I was on I-10, I turned on my radar detector and kicked the turbo Porsche up to over 100 mph, and lost whatever tail they might have put on me. So far, it was just a business game for them. I wanted the millions that they owed me, and they tried to screw me out of it to save a multi-million payout. For that kind of money, they could be expected to do just about anything to avoid payment.

My first stop was a post office near Osborn Plaza in Scottsdale, where I rented a PO Box for a year. The next stop was the Department of Motor Vehicles, on East Paradise Lane, where I applied for an Arizona driver's license.

I spent the night in nearby Gainey Ranch at the Hyatt Regency. I awoke early the next morning and went for a quick five-mile run before the heat became unbearable.

An hour later, I stopped in at Gainey Guns and Ammo and talked to Bud, whose identification badge indicated he was the manager.

"I want to purchase four guns. I want your recommendations for a concealed carry gun; a high capacity 9mm automatic; a quality AR 15 type weapon and a 12-gauge shotgun."

Bud didn't hesitate. "That should work," he said, nodding his head, as he started pulling weapons out of the display cases and placing them on the counter in front of me.

"This first one is called a Heizer, Double Tap," he said as he cleared the weapon to confirm it wasn't loaded. "It is amazing. Just about the smallest carry gun on the market. Its caliper is both 45ACP and 410 together and fires two rounds. It can also hold an additional two backup rounds."

"Isn't a 410 a shotgun round?"

"Yup, it is," he replied. "That's what so sweet about this weapon. It takes either round or both. I would recommend loading it with two 410 shells and then store two 45s in its handle. If there is anything left after firing the 410s, you've got the 45s for a reload. This is strictly a close-range firearm."

He had it in three different finishes. I chose titanium. He set it aside on the counter and cleared the magazine on a different weapon, and then handed it over to me.

"This is a Para Pro Custom 18.9. It is really nice. It is a 9MM. It carries 18 rounds and comes with fiber optic sights and a match-quality barrel. It is hard to miss with this beauty."

I nodded my head, and he pushed the Para over by the Heizer and reached up and grabbed a weapon off a wall mount.

"This is a custom AR 15 from Wilson Combat. The caliper is a 7.62X40 WT for minimal recoil. The fellow who ordered this left the area, so it is yours if you want it. They don't come any better."

I hefted the weapon, and after a quick adjustment of stock length, it fit perfectly. It was very similar to the weapon I had used and was familiar with in the Gulf.

I spent another hour getting set up with holsters, gun cases, and enough ammo to practice and defeat a small banana republic army.

The 12-gauge shotgun was right off the shelf---a 500 SPX Mossberg. I presented my new driver's license and paid in cash. In Arizona, I could buy guns and walk out the door with them. In California, I would have run into all sorts of problems, from the size of the magazines to the waiting period before I could pick up the guns. I knew what they meant when they said---"I would rather be judged by 12, then carried by 6.

I also signed up for the concealed carry class that was being offered the following day.

~ ~***~ ~

With my freshly printed concealed carry permit, I headed back to San Diego. I stopped right before the California border in a little town called Ehrenberg, Arizona, and headed out into the boonies to familiarize myself with my new toys. An hour later and after several hundred rounds of ammo, I found that they all checked out just fine. I have to admit that my hand still stung from the kick of firing several 410-shotgun rounds through the little Heizer Double Tap. I guess it suited its purpose. Anybody or anything on the receiving end of the weapon would know that they had just been trampled by a herd of wild elephants.

21

• • • • • • • • • • • • • •

Bugs – The electronic kind

During the next two weeks, we started sending out dozens of subpoenas for possible depositions in and around Biloxi, Mississippi.

A typical day for me, during this period, consisted of a long run in the morning before daylight. Then I would drive to Kiddrick's office in San Diego and work with him and one of his junior partners, David Stone, gathering documents and creating potential questions for each person being deposed. Later, I would head back to the Fairbanks Ranch sales office and work for the rest of the afternoon and early evening.

Every day I noticed, or at least I thought I did, different people following me, from my home to Kiddrick's office and then while driving back to Fairbanks again.

After the first two days of this, I called Ralph Landers, the former sheriff and polygraph man who I had used previously when I was fired. I asked him to come to my new home in Fairbanks Ranch and sweep for bugs.

The following day, I met with Ralph. "Well, Sam, I have been doing these kinds of inspections for years, and quite honestly, I didn't know what to expect at your home. The security in Fairbanks is excellent. I used to work with several members of their guard patrol when they were deputies. The gates are always locked and secured, and the guests and homeowners have to have the correct documents in their car windows, or they get pulled over and checked."

"I know Ralph, I'm the one who set up a lot the security procedures here. We needed the best to compete with the best."

"Well, it has been compromised. Someone got into the community and bypassed your own security at your house and filled it with high-tech equipment. Whoever did it were experts of the highest order. I'm pretty sure I got everything, but it wasn't easy. They had pinhole cameras throughout your home, and if you whispered anywhere in the house, they could pick you up on their mics."

"Fabulous. Talk about feeling violated. What do think would have happened if Jenny or Mikey had shown up unexpected while they were doing this?"

"Well, frankly, they could have been shot. The goons who we arrested a couple of years ago, monitoring your house, who were former FBI, are probably long gone. Southern could be using a different class of thugs now."

"I'm glad I had you check."

"I would hate to think what could have happened. These guys are playing for keeps, it seems. The good news, if there can be any, is that everything looked newly installed, not more than a couple of weeks old. I reported it to Fairbanks security, and they have agreed to patrol your home several more times each day than they normally do. After Jenny left for work this morning, I had some of my guys come in and beef up your security system to the highest commercial grade available. Other than that, I don't know what more to suggest."

"Should we call the police and see if we can have someone arrested at Southern? Nobody else would be interested in bugging my place."

Landers shook his head. "We can't prove they had anything to do with this. The spy stuff that they installed in your house was either wiped for prints, or the parts were too small to even get a partial. This was top dollar stuff. I have reported the break-in to the sheriff's department, and they had a crew out to look for prints, but I don't expect to find any, other than your own family."

The next day I arranged for Landers and his crew to come to Kiddrick's law offices and perform a similar search. The results were identical.

Kiddrick went ballistic when he was told of the results of the search. He made a few phone calls and then asked for Landers and me to join him across the street at the courthouse for a quick meeting with the Presiding Judge of the San Diego Superior Court.

As we rode up in the elevator to the judge's chambers, Kiddrick smiled and chuckled a few times to himself without explanation.

We entered the chambers, and Kiddrick quickly changed his demeanor to one of stoic anger as he introduced us to Judge Emil Sorenson. He took the bag of spy gear from Landers and then asked for us to wait outside the room for him while he talked with the judge.

Less than five minutes later, Kiddrick came out into the hallway and motioned us to be quiet and follow him back across the street to his office. He whistled softly, almost to himself, on his way to his conference room, where he motioned for David to join us. He sat there, smiling as he waited for us to get seated.

"What did I miss? I asked, looking directly at Ben.

"Oh, you mean the anger and then the whistling?" he replied. I whistle when I'm happy---and I whistle when the enemy makes a mistake. Southern made a big mistake. Nobody can probably prove it inside a courtroom, but outside there is little doubt that these guys are just everyday thugs. They can wear three-piece suits and work for a Fortune 500 Company, but they are still just thugs, and they will eventually pay for it. It is also one thing to bug a private residence, but it is totally a different game if they violate the sanctity of an officer of the court. They have broken a cardinal sin."

"Okay, what does that mean for us? You said there was 'little doubt,' that means there was some doubt.'"

"The way I read it, Judge Sorenson is fairly confident that Southern has broken the rules big time. He will meet with the judge assigned to our trial and voice his concerns. You have to understand that when a court case is worth millions of dollars, people will often do just about anything to win. The judge doesn't know you from Adam. He has to also consider that you may have planted the bugs in your own home and my office to throw suspicion their way. Fortunately, Judge Sorenson and I have known each other for more than thirty years---we even went to Berkley together. He knows I wouldn't bug my own office."

We arranged for Landers to sweep both my home and Kiddrick's office on a continuing but random basis until the trial started.

22

. . . .

Playing with fire

My new schedule became hectic. Not only did I have to be on call for Kiddrick, but I also still had to perform my management and sales duties at Fairbanks Ranch.

Mickey called me one evening and arranged to meet me the following morning in Phase 3, located in the northeastern section of our project. We needed to take one of the off-road jeeps that had four-wheel drive, to get to where we needed to work.

We had to walk several of the lots to verify the correct grading results and create the new pricing schedule for the latest phase to be released for sale.

This was dirty work. We were both dressed in jeans and boots and were expected to walk every lot from corner to corner. We traveled up and down the graded areas and through the brush to the next adjoining lot. We were both hot and sweating after a couple of hours of this work.

I think Mickey thought I was kidding when I told him to freeze and not move at all.

The boom from the little Heizer was enough to scare an average person to death. To Mickey, it was just another noise that had saved him from a painful trip to the hospital.

Rattlesnake splatter was all over the place. Little chunks of blood and intestines were still moving in a final nerve reaction.

"Didn't see that one did I." Mickey shook his head in wonder. "That's twice now. What did you shoot him with, a bazooka?"

I showed him the little Double Tap and then put it back in my pocket.

"Have you ever mistaken that for a cigarette lighter? Remind me not to ever smoke around you."

A few minutes later, we heard the sounds of sirens, and I assumed someone had phoned in a report of gunshots. I was wrong.

When we returned to the office, there was a crowd of people, two fire trucks, and a $130,000 red turbo Porsche fully engulfed in flames. My little red turbo Porsche.

Again, no one could prove it was Southern who torched my car. The police said it could have been anyone. Someone had dropped a bottle full of gasoline through my half-open sunroof and had ignited it. There were no witnesses. It didn't take a genius to figure out that the fire was a warning. This time, no one was hurt. Would I be so lucky next time? I had to share this news with Jenny. She did not take it well.

I replaced the red Porsche with a large, white Hummer. I was getting ready to go to war.

A couple of years after getting out of the Marine Corps, I had signed up and attended grad school at Pepperdine University. The classes were made up of adults in their twenties and thirties. Several of my classmates were affiliated with law enforcement. I say affiliated because some of them were members of one of those mysterious alphabet companies like DEA, FBI, CIA, and various Federal task forces.

Literally, one the nicest guys in the group was a contract killer for the CIA. Al would fly in behind enemy lines---do a HALO drop, kill a village chief and then be extricated, and be back in class 48 hours later.

One day during our lunch break, the usually cheerful Al was unusually quiet and morose. I asked him what was bothering him. In brief, his younger sister was being deported from the United States because her visa had expired. She needed to secure a good-paying job if she wished to remain here in the U.S. permanently.

I asked Al if I could meet her and see if I could figure out a way to help her. To make a long story short, I made a few phone calls and called in a favor and was able to get her a well-paying job at Washington Mutual.

The next time Al and I talked over lunch, he said he owed me. I laughed and told him he could buy our lunch. We were eating at In-N-Out Burgers. He paid for lunch, and I thought we were even.

Al pulled me aside before we went back into the classroom. "Sam, you know what I do for a living. If you ever need something like that done, I'll do it, no questions asked. I really do owe you."

I explained that I was happy to help him out, but he wouldn't drop it. Even after we graduated, he would remind me of his promise from time to time. I never took him up on it---until now.

I called Al from a payphone near Cardiff by the Sea. I don't know if you have checked lately, but payphones are not that easy to find anymore. They are about as common as unicorns.

He picked up right away. "Are you calling about the payback we discussed? If so, call me at the following number in ten minutes from a payphone."

He gave me the number, then hung up.

Ten minutes later, he picked up the phone on the first ring and laughed as I asked if his payback promise was still any good. "Payback is good at any time," he replied. "Who do you want me to terminate?"

"Can I request something a little less permanent?" I asked quietly.

"Absolutely, payback is payback. What or *who* do you need done?"

"A not so nice gentleman in Texas blew up my car yesterday. He is a multi-billionaire and thinks he can get away with just about anything. I just thought that it might be only fair to blow up his car, exactly the same way mine was done"

"I like how you think," Al said.

We spent the next several minutes discussing who the target was and where he was located. I requested that a bottle of gasoline be dropped into his car and somehow be ignited, just like they had done to my car.

He told me that unless he told me otherwise, to plan on being surrounded by people on Saturday night.

On Sunday morning, it was reported on the Huffington Post website that there had been a car explosion at the estate of the Democratic vice chairman in Houston, Texas. It said that a car belonging to the Chairman of Southern Industries, Jack Blackwell, was totally destroyed in the fire. The car was late model Cornish, Rolls Royce valued at more than $300,000. Investigators were considering it a case of arson.

23

* * * * * * * * * * * * * *

Discovery

A few days later, David Stone, Ben's junior partner and I traveled to Mississippi for our first round of depositions. David was young, aggressive, and looking forward to pinning Southern Industries to the wall. Ben explained to me that David would represent their firm on this first trip. He would do a super job, and he would be considerably less expensive on my wallet. He then gave me his opinion on the discovery process.

"A good series of depositions can help discover everything we need to know prior to trial. We want to find out where the smoking guns are so that we are not surprised when you testify in court. David will ask numerous questions that he would typically not be allowed to ask in court. Once they answer a question, it becomes part of the trial documents. If they change their answer in court several months from now, we can try and show that they lied to us either in the deposition or in court.

"Do you know what the difference is between a chronic liar and someone who is caught in a lie only once?

Nothing. Either way, they are both considered liars---and hopefully, they will lose all credibility with the court."

~ ~***~ ~

We left Lindberg Field in the mid-morning, changed planes in Denver, and then flew directly to Mobile, Alabama, a trip I had made several times in the past.

From the airport in Mobile, we rented a car and drove off, headed back west down Highway 10, and eventually turned off on Interstate 110 heading south to Biloxi.

We checked into The Hard Rock Hotel and Casino on Beach Blvd across the street from the Gulf of Mexico. It was a typically miserable day on the Gulf Coast. The humidity had to be close to 90%, and the temperature was almost as high. In the late afternoons, they were experiencing massive thunder and lightning storms. Everything smelled like it was rotting and decaying around us. Why did it remind me of Hong Kong?

It wasn't my first choice for a hotel, but it was clean, fresh and they were offering their rooms at a 50% discount to keep their casino area full. After British Petroleum had damaged miles of coastline with one of the most significant oil spills in U.S. history, many of the casinos were fighting to stay in business.

It had been a long day to that point, and we both agreed to get some sleep before we began our depositions the following day.

I had been carrying the little Heizer Double Tap for the past several weeks wherever I went. I had been followed continuously for the last three weeks since my car had been destroyed. Because of the plane travel---required for this trip, I was forced to leave the weapon at home. Even the little Heizer couldn't get past a TSA inspection.

Now that we were in Southern's and Clem Garland's home territory, I felt naked without it.

24

· · · · · · · · · · · · · · · ·

The belly of the beast

We arrived precisely on time at Southern's Mississippi branch headquarters. David was dressed in his lawyer uniform of gray slacks, a white Oxford dress shirt, and club tie finished off with a dark blue blazer. I was dressed casual, in light tan slacks and a green polo golf shirt with a Fairbanks Ranch Country Club logo over the pocket. I'm not sure of my intentions for going so casual. Subconsciously, I was either looking for the *I don't give a damn if everyone else is wearing suits and ties look,* or I just wanted them to know that they were of little concern to me, and because of my lack of respect for them, I would dress however I pleased. Besides, you have to be somewhat crazy to wear a suit in this hot, humid area of the country.

The receptionist greeted us cordially and asked if we had an appointment. She acted as though we were there to repair the Xerox machine.

I felt like replying that we had an appointment for the last two years, and we were here to collect, but I behaved myself.

She returned to her typing and phone duties while she munched on a monster cinnamon roll covered with glazed sugar. What? I can't even imagine a secretary in health-conscious California eating this colossal pile of calories and grease in public view. They might eat it in the break room or under their desk, but in public---no.

She had us wait for nearly twenty minutes before finally guiding us back to a small conference room near the executive offices. There were three or four lawyers present, a female court recorder and Garland himself with a crazy smirk on his face. They sat together at a long, beat-up looking Formica covered conference table, surrounded by cheap plastic chairs.

Most of the attorneys and, of course, Garland were smoking cigarettes, which was creating a dense fog of contaminants that hung over the room.

They all acted like they were terribly inconvenienced and annoyed that we would be interrupting their typical workday. They were even more annoyed when David requested that they extinguish their coffin nails so that we could proceed with the depositions.

The attorneys had previously agreed to allow us to depose three people the first day. The second day we would have full access to their records for Leisure PT, which they had not provided during the initial discovery requests.

After the first deposition, Garland turned his head towards his lawyers and started to laugh.

"Something funny, Clem?" I asked.

Garland just shook his head. "I was just thinking about how much this lawsuit must be costing ya. You might need to rob a bank before you leave town." He continued to chuckle while his attorney friends joined in.

"You're right---this is going to be an expensive trip. Rather than rob a bank, it probably would be a lot easier for me to play some more golf with you. That's almost like robbing a bank."

On that uplifting note, David called the next witness.

I did learn at least two important things about depositions. No one knows more about the facts of a case than the plaintiffs and the defendants. Several times I noticed that David had asked a good question but then would fail to follow-up on it because he simply did not know the business. I asked David to take a short recess while I went back to the front reception desk. After an annoying conversation with Miss Cinnabon, I purchased a pad of Post-it Notes for $20, several times what it was worth, but I felt it was necessary.

I soon found that if I paid close attention to the person being deposed, they rarely told a lie. It was one thing to fill out a questionnaire about what happened concerning a certain question. It was totally another case when I was sitting directly across from them, waiting for them to explain the same question. As silly as it sounds, whenever someone would start to lie about something, if I stared hard at them and minutely shook my head, they would change their story and tell the truth. Remarkable.

Throughout the next deposition, I would scratch out a quick question for David to ask, tear it off the pad, and then stick it in front of him. At first, everyone but David thought it was funny until we started nailing them on things from which they were not prepared. From that point on, they would grimace when they noticed me preparing another question.

After another two hours, we called it a day and returned to our hotel.

When we arrived the next day, we were advised that the hard copy records, we were to examine, were being kept in their basement, which was without adequate air conditioning. The AC unit had broken the previous day (surprise, surprise), and they would be unable to get it fixed this week.

Mississippi, in the dead of summer, was steamy hot. Within three minutes of walking outside into the daylight, your clothes would stick to your skin.

When I asked if they could bring their records upstairs for us to examine, they stated that the documents were kept in large filing cabinets, and they could not be moved. If that wasn't satisfactory, we could just pass on the records and move on to the next depositions. On several occasions, they indicated that there wasn't anything of importance to us in the hard copy files that had not already been passed on to us in computer files.

They seemed to overplay the lack of the need to examine their hard files. No matter if they were located in a rat-infested sauna, we had to look through those files.

We were guided to their basement by one of Garland's attorneys, and we were introduced to a hot secretary (a play on words intended) wearing the thinnest of sundresses, who maintained the files for the entire floor. There was also a blue-uniformed guard who was already soaking through his shirt, displaying massive sweat stains. They would supervise the files that we were allowed to have access to throughout the day.

They led us down a dark aisle until we came to a bank of black file cabinets and a long table that was illuminated by floodlights. The lights were necessary to read the documents, but they also added to the exhaustive heat.

The first nine rows of file cabinets had yellow tape stuck across their top drawers indicated which files we were to be allowed access. There were an additional three rows, but we were told that we did not have access to those and that they had nothing to do with the Leisure PT. I was surprised that they didn't have flashing Christmas lights on them, indicating that if we were going to find anything of interest, they would be in these cabinets. David looked over at me, and I avoided his look as if everything was fine.

The attorney gave final instructions to everyone.

David and I were to be supervised at all times by the guard. If we wanted to investigate any of the file cabinet drawers, we were to ask the guard. After getting the key from the secretary, he would unlock drawers for us. They rolled in a copying machine and set it up next to our work desk, and we were allowed to copy as much as we wanted at a cost of 25 cents per page. *Seriously.*

For the next three hours, David and I worked on the first four of the eight file cabinets. As expected, there was nothing of value in any of these cabinets.

Within the first hour, the sweaty and bored rent-a-cop started thinking up any excuse to wander three rows over to talk with the secretary. We noticed right away that when we requested him to open one of the cabinets, he would go to the secretary for the key. As soon as he opened it, he would return the key to her and spend several more minutes talking with her.

When he returned after one of these visits, I asked him how long had he and the secretary had been dating.

He looked shocked for a moment before responding. "We're not dating," he said, his cheeks slowly turning pink.

"Really," I responded. "You look perfect together. I thought you might be a couple."

He thought about it for a couple of minutes. "I wouldn't mind dating her. But I've only seen her a couple of times before."

"What did she say when you asked her out?"

His blush returned as he replied, "I've never asked her out. I don't know if she would go with me."

"Really? How do you know that, if you've never asked her? She seems like she's really interested in you, the way she was looking at you when you weren't looking."

"She was looking at me?"

"Either at you or your gun. She was definitely looking in your direction."

He considered that for a moment. "Girls do love guns, ya know?"

"Where are you two going for lunch today when we take our break?"

"What do you mean?"

"The quickest way for you to find out if she is interested in you is to ask her out. Since you're both working together today, what better excuse could there be?"

"But, we're supposed to watch you today."

"We've got to eat too. We won't be here, besides you've got the keys. We can't open any more cabinets without them unless you would rather go to lunch with us. You know, just the three of us?"

"Let me check with her, and I'll be right back."

A few minutes later, he came back beaming. "She said, yes! We're going to lunch together!"

David gathered his papers and put them in his briefcase and then made a production about leaving. "Sam, I'm going to go upstairs and see if a couple of the other lawyers want to go to lunch with us. Are you coming?"

"I've got one more file to do, then, I'll join you."

David left, and the guard started nervously checking his watch every couple of minutes. I continued to work on as if I had all of the time in the world.

After another fifteen minutes, the guard couldn't take it any longer. "Sir, how much more time do you need?"

"Is there a problem?"

"No, of course not, it's just---I promised I would take Brittany to lunch. She's probably ready to blow me off now. I promised we would leave in a few minutes."

"I am so sorry," I said earnestly. "I forgot all about your date. Look, get going. I'm fine. I need to spend a few more minutes on this file, and then I am done for the day. You can probably take a two-hour lunch, and nobody would be the wiser. In fact, here, take the file and lock it away. I just need to make a few more copies, and I'm out of here."

He almost ran over to the secretary's desk, got the keys, and locked the remaining files away.

"Thanks, sir. She waited for me. If I don't see you again, thanks for the advice. We're going to have a great lunch."

I waited for about five minutes and then went over to the secretary's desk and opened the top drawer. The file cabinet keys were right there in the pencil tray.

Within minutes I opened the file cabinets--- the ones we were not supposed to have access to and found an amazing amount of records that should have been burned weeks ago. I made copies of everything of importance and replaced them in the files and kept the originals. These guys were so lazy they couldn't spend an additional hour cleaning out their cabinets and destroying anything that might be detrimental to their lawsuit.

David and I had a productive lunch at a local eatery and determined our new game plan.

When we returned to Southern, David talked briefly with the opposing counsel. In the interest of brevity, he suggested that if we could depose their in-house counsel, who happened to be present right now, we would only take a few more minutes of their time and finish up with Garland's deposition in the morning. David indicated that we were finished with the file cabinets and would not need them any longer. They were jubilant to hear this.

The one concern that was voiced by all of the attorneys, was that the counsel would not be badgered into violating any attorney-client privilege. That was agreed upon, and we proceeded.

~ ~***~ ~

A smug-looking William Jefferies, in-house counsel for Southern's regional office in Mississippi, was sworn in and shifted around in his chair until he was comfortable.

After several minutes of fundamental questioning regarding Jefferies credentials and working relationship with SI, David got to the meat of the deposition.

"Mr. Jefferies, are you familiar with the files that Sam Barns and I examined this morning, in this office?"

"I am."

"How familiar are you with these documents?"

"Very."

"Can you provide us with more details on that?"

"I can. Clem, I mean, Mr. Garland, and I took it upon ourselves to personally sort through all of the pertinent files of Leisure PT, and made them available for your inspection today or for however how long you need to examine them."

"When you say sort, you mean you examined each and every document, leaving out only those that were not pertinent to the Leisure PT litigation? Is that your testimony?"

"It is indeed my testimony."

I scribbled a quick question to David and stuck it on the desk in front of him.

"Are you, sir, familiar with the litigation issues filed by Mr. Barns against Southern and their counter-suit litigation issues filed back against him?"

"Am I answering this question from you or from Mr. Sticky-Doo?" he asked sarcastically. "You know that is very annoying."

"Be that as it may," replied David, "you need to answer any reasonable question that I ask you, truthfully and to the best of your knowledge."

He asked for the question to be repeated again.

"I am. I helped write the counter-suit."

"Just to be clear for the record, you and Mr. Garland personally examined each and every file requested by your opposing counsel, and fulfilled their requests to the best of your abilities. Is that a correct statement?"

"It is," Jefferies responded with a bored expression on his face.

"Sir, I'm going to hand you what we will label as exhibits A through F. I want you to start with exhibit A and explain the document for the record. Is that agreeable?"

"It is."

David passed the stack to the court recorder, who labeled the exhibits, kept a copy for herself, and returned a copy to Jackson and David.

I watched closely as Jefferies looked at exhibit A, and then started coughing. He took a drink of water, rested a moment, and then took another sip.

"Sir, are you alright? We can take an extra moment if you like. Just let me know."

Jefferies waved him off as he frantically examined exhibits B through F. Another spasm of coughing took hold of him.

"Mr. Jefferies, can you describe exhibit A to me? The one described as *Balance Sheet Actuals*. I checked with my home office over the lunch break, and they emailed me back your previously submitted Exhibit B, which is labeled as *Balance Sheet, Leisure PT*. The best that I can tell is that they both cover the same period of time, but the numbers are extraordinarily different. Can you tell me why that is, sir?"

"Where did you get these papers?" wheezed Jefferies as he stood up.

"Mr. Barns found them in some file cabinets downstairs. Is it your testimony that you are not familiar with these documents? You don't recognize any of them?"

Jefferies looked menacingly at me and then at David. "Fuck both of you. That's my testimony," he said as he grabbed his briefcase and exited the conference room.

25

- - - - - - - - - - - - - - -

Mississippi – After dark

That night, back in his hotel room, David received a strange phone call. When we had checked in together at the Hard Rock, they had mistakenly listed his room in my name. At the time we thought nothing of it and continued to our respective rooms.

A whispered voice told David that he had information that could blow SI right out of the water. He asked if *I* could meet him in the Wynn Dixie parking lot, just off of Highway 90, the following night at midnight. David assured him that I would be there.

David, of course, called me right away and passed on the message. He joked about us having our own Mississippi *Deep Throat*. "Our depositions today must have shaken up a few people. Now we have someone who wants to be on our side. The rats are abandoning their ship."

I tossed and turned in my bed, thinking about this possible break. There was no way I was going to sleep this night. I got out of my bed and changed into my running gear.

The moon was a silvery, waning crescent a few inches off the horizon, as I looked out over the Gulf. It was barely enough light to avoid stepping into an uneven section of the beach and breaking a leg.

If you're a runner, you have to learn to deal with it.

After twenty minutes of running on the beach, I was sure of two things. I was sick of being in hot, miserable Mississippi, surrounded by thieves, and that someone had been following me since I left the hotel.

I have been followed for the past two or three years, so this wasn't an entirely new experience. It was a concern, though, that unlike the past, I was in Southern's backyard. They had been flagrant in their efforts to follow me. It was as if they wanted me to know they were around and could cause me problems anytime they desired. They tried to keep the pressure on me and wanted me to see that I was making a big mistake pursuing this lawsuit. They were big important guys, and they wanted me to be fully aware of it. They could squash me at any moment if they so chose.

Even at this time of the night, there were a few people on the beach. A couple strolling, holding hands, teenagers smoking cigarettes and vaping---huddled together around a small fire pit that had been dug into the sand.

Rows of tall, drooping trees lined the area between the land and the sandy beach. The moon looked as though it belonged on a Russian flag, providing just enough light to make out shapes, but little else.

I increased my running pace, and I could hear my possible pursuer fall back gasping for air. Within a few seconds, he was no longer a concern. Twenty-five minutes more and I made my turn back towards the hotel---an easy up and back route.

My mind tends to wander when I run. My legs run mechanically correct, and my arms keep a simple rhythm. Nothing really cerebral is going on, so I think about my current problems and my strategies to resolve them. At least that's what I was doing when I noticed the man coming out of the trees to my left, who began jogging towards me as if he too were out for a run.

Dressed in dark clothing, with a knit cap pulled down to his eyebrows, on this hot and humid evening, something was obviously amiss. If I hadn't felt that I was being followed earlier in the evening, I probably would have just dismissed it. There were a lot of strange joggers in the world, and Mississippi was no exception.

He continued jogging towards me with his head down, running at a very slow pace. His current path would take him past me at about four feet to my left side. I readied myself mentally for an attack as he passed me, but he kept on jogging.

Before I could relax again, I heard a scuff in the sand behind me, and a hand grabbed my left shoulder to turn me around. In a split second, I saw the jogger with a shiny object in his hand, swinging it up towards my chest. Training is everything. Without a moment's hesitation, I continued to turn towards him---the natural reaction is to pull away. My right leg kicked out and made solid contact with his left knee, which was probably supporting 90% of his weight. The sickening sound of breaking bone and cartilage, followed by a cry of pain, disrupted the evening silence. The knife, in the middle of an upward arc, stopped in mid-flight and fell to the ground with the rest of his body.

He cursed loudly and tried to get up. Without a moment's hesitation, I kicked him again, this time on the side of the head, enough to make him unconscious, but probably not enough to kill him.

I know what you're thinking. In a fair fight, you're not supposed to kick people in the head. You're also not supposed to kick someone when their down---forget it. This wasn't supposed to be a fair fight. He was probably trying to kill me. In a movie, the good guy would lean over and pick up the bad guy by the front of his shirt, and by twisting the material really hard, he would get a confession---and then we would break for a commercial. Not so in real life. Any martial arts instructor will explain to you the simple rules of engagement. If given the opportunity, always strike first and use any means to take out your opponent. In truth, good guys do indeed finish last. It was one of the first lessons I learned in the Marine Corp.

I touched my index and middle finger to the side of his neck and felt for a pulse. It was weak but fast, as it should be. I rolled him over onto his back.

I picked up his knife, folded the blade, and held on to it as I searched through the rest of his clothing. The two pockets in his sweatpants were empty. No wallet, identification, or a room key. He needed a haircut, and he smelled like he might work on a fishing boat.

I was about to stand up when I noticed that his sweatshirt also had a pouch in the front.

The gun was a Ruger 22/45 lite, with a noise suppressor screwed into its barrel. Any doubt I may have had, that this was intended to be a simple mugging, vanished. The gun with a silencer made him a professional, a dumb one at that. If he had been smart, he would have simply run up to me and shot me in the forehead and be back in his room already, packing his bags. Instead, he was lying on the beach with a broken knee and a concussion. I kicked him again in the head, to ensure he would be out of commission during our stay in Mississippi. His concussion was now a severe concussion. He would have a headache that he would remember for several more weeks and a limp that would last a lifetime. I was probably too nice to him.

I continued jogging down the beach until I got to the pier. I threw the knife as far out in the water as I could and kept the gun. After tonight I just might need it for our meeting with *Deep Throat* the following evening.

When I reached the hotel, I went up to my room, got some change, went back down to the lobby, and made an anonymous call to the police from a payphone. I told them there was a rapist on the beach that was getting beaten up by a group of men.

The last the thing I wanted to do was talk to the police in Mississippi. Garland was probably commander of their local neighborhood watch program.

26

· · · · · · · · · · · · · · ·

Belly of the beast – Day 3

The next day during Garland's deposition, he answered several of our questions truthfully, while having a terrible memory on just about everything else.

He was not a happy camper this morning. His team seemed to be letting him down. Someone would pay for these mistakes.

His standard answer for most of the questions was to first ask the stenographer to repeat the question, often several times. He would then hesitate for several more minutes and then admit that he could not recall the facts surrounding the question.

He only got angry near the end of the deposition when we questioned him several times about the documents that I had found in the locked file cabinets. He swore that he knew nothing of the paperwork, and that the attorney had been working by himself, and that he was not present during any discussions of the files.

He looked over at me at one point and stared angrily. "So tell me, Sam, where did you find those papers? I've never seen them before."

I looked at him and smiled. "You'll have to ask me that during my deposition. Oh, that's right, I already had my deposition. I guess it is your turn right now."

While David and one of the opposing attorneys were working with the court reporter on numbering the exhibits, Garland looked over at me and smiled. "So how is Mr. Sticky-Doo today? Cheating anybody at golf?"

"Asshole," I said quietly. "There's no need to cheat at golf in Mississippi. I heard that Ray Charles was your club champion." I know it was childish of me but well worth the satisfaction of seeing the look on his face when I said it.

~ ~***~ ~

That evening, David and I drove over to the Wynn Dixie parking lot for our mystery meeting with Deep Throat. I had examined the gun from the previous night, and it was locked and loaded and resting comfortably in my hand as we pulled into the empty parking lot.

We waited nearly forty minutes for the arrival of Deep Throat. When no one arrived at the appointed hour, we assumed "deep throat" was lying in a hospital room, somewhere local, with his leg in a cast, and hopefully in a coma.

If it was the same man who attacked me on the beach, I'm sure his name was Mud to whoever had hired him.

27

● ● ● ● ● ● ● ● ● ● ● ● ● ●

Happiness is Texas
in my review mirror

The next few weeks went by like a bullet. We held a dozen more depositions all over the country, but they yielded very few new hard facts that might be useful for our upcoming trial.

Back in San Diego, we gathered at Kiddrick's office for a much-needed strategy secession. We had received only a handful of good breaks in the evidence chain. Southern had professionals shredding files 24/7, and my claims were becoming just that---unsubstantiated claims. It was going to be my words against a Fortune 500 company. Even though we had discovered incriminating files at Southern's Mississippi headquarters, it was only one or two points against them, they still had several more areas against me that would be hard to prove, one way or another.

"I've got an idea," I said, during a break in the conversation.

Kiddrick nodded his head towards me and motioned for me to continue.

"We need to depose Jack Blackwell," I said. "He's the weak link. The others will lie to protect themselves, while Jack is so damn arrogant, he'll try to outsmart us."

Kiddrick shook his head before responding. "It's really a stretch to depose him. All of your dealings were with Randall and Garland. I doubt that we could depose him---just because he's the Chairman of Southern. Bill Gates would always be in court if he was required to attend every lawsuit that involved Microsoft."

I shook my head. "I made my decision to sell out to Southern Industries based upon my meetings with Jack, and his stability and honesty as a chief executive of that company. If SI was involved with fixed books and threats, the orders had to come from Blackwell. Randall continually told me his orders came directly from the top, that being Jack Blackwell. Believe me, you will never meet a man more arrogant and annoying. If anyone is going to give us a needed break, it would have to be him."

Kiddrick smiled grimly and then nodded his head in agreement. "That should be good enough for the court. David---have him served immediately and book your flights for Houston. It will probably be the only chance we will have to talk with him. There's very little chance that he will leave Texas and come to California for the trial. He can't be forced to come to California. We should run that sucker through the wringer if we get the chance."

Two weeks later, we were on a Delta flight headed for Texas. SI had changed and canceled Blackwell's deposition twice because he was such a busy and important guy. David had retained a court reporter for the deposition from a local service in Houston and confirmed again that they had reserved a conference room at Southern's headquarters.

We settled back in our seats, ordered a couple of Diet Cokes as David retrieved his briefcase from under the seats in front of us.

While David prepared a list of questions for Blackwell, I was thumbing my way through the airline's reading materials, found in the seatback. I started reading an article about new practices in law. Halfway through the article, I put down the magazine.

"David, have you heard anything about a law that allows you to video record depositions?"

David looked up from his notes and nodded his head. "Yeah, it's been allowed for a while now. The courts decided that anything could happen to an out-of-state transcript, and it could be costly, to say the least, if it was not recoverable or accurate."

"Let's do it," I replied. "Jack has such an ego---he might not know how to act in front of a camera. When I've met with him in the past, he constantly touches his hair, to assure himself that everything is in place, and he often makes strange faces as if testing his facial muscles. He might come across as strange. It's at least worth a try. It might be the only opportunity for a jury in California to see this jerk in action. What do we have to lose?"

"Good point," said David with a concerned smile. "It's worth a try."

We called from the airplane and ordered a camera and tripod to be delivered to Southern's offices.

Upon departing the plane in Houston, we were again shocked after leaving the air-conditioned coolness of the plane and being met on the off-ramp with 100-degree weather and 90% humidity.

When we arrived at SI's headquarters, we found that someone had canceled the court reporter. We arranged for another replacement reporter, and the deposition was postponed for an hour. No surprise there. They had been behaving this way for almost three years now.

In the conference room, I set up the VCR camera while David went through his notes. The room was about the size of our main office back at Leisure PT. Several gray suits meandered into the room and took their places on the opposite side of the enormous conference table.

The room was decorated more like a hunting lodge in Vermont than a business office in Texas. No expense had been spared. The table was at least twenty to thirty feet long. The comfortable chairs were made from luxurious, polished walnut with the seats crafted from real, almost chocolate-colored leather.

I guess that's how they decorate in billion-dollar companies.

Southern's in-house lead attorney told David that they would be ready to begin as soon as Blackwell was finished with an urgent conference call.

By this point in time, I had been involved in nearly fifty depositions. I knew the mechanics, many of the tricks, and when to object. I also knew that I was the only one that was aware of all nuances of the case. Based on my experience in Mississippi, I had several notepads of 3M Post-it stickers to write messages to David.

The door opened abruptly, and a polished-looking Jack Blackwell entered the conference room. I had been impressed with Randall's three-piece business suits. Jack made him look like a pauper. All of his staff stood up immediately as if the king of England had just entered the room.

The air in the conference room seemed electrified.

Jack motioned for them to sit down and then glared across the table at David and me like an angry ferret. While David ignored his rudeness, I returned his glare.

His counsel leaned next to him to whisper something in his ear, but he brushed him away like a nuisance and continued to glare at us. He maintained the presence of a dictator. He snapped his cuffs, straightened his perfect tie, and unconsciously smoothed back his hair to near perfection.

"Alright," Jack said. "Let's get this going. I don't have much time for you. I have a busy schedule today."

David smiled over at him and nodded his head. "I'm sure you do Mr. Blackwell, but we will take as long as we need to depose you today and maybe even tomorrow if we want."

As Jack started rising out of his chair, his counsel put his hand on his arm and whispered into his ear. Blackwell returned to his seat, fuming.

"While the reporter swears in Mr. Blackwell---Sam, why don't you set up the camera so that we're ready to begin?"

I lifted the camera and its tripod off of the floor, next to me, and set it up directly across from Blackwell and began recording.

Again, Jack was out of his seat and screaming across the table. "What's this bullshit? I'm not allowing you to take movies of me while I'm testifying. You can fuck yourselves."

His counsel again whispered to him, and he shook his head several times before he returned to his seat. His forehead was glossy wet with sweat, and he loosened his necktie.

"As your counsel has no doubt advised you, Mr. Blackwell, we have every legal right to record this deposition on camera. I'm sorry if this is uncomfortable for you. Let's begin."

"Please pronounce and spell your entire name for the court record."

"This is bullshit," Blackwell replied. "You know who I am. Let's get on with it."

David smiled pleasantly and then continued. "Call it what you might---we've got all the time in the world for you to respond, but we need your response."

Blackwell said his name and then stopped and looked over at the camera. "I'm not saying another word until you get rid of the damn flashing red light on that thing!"

Without comment, I reached over and put a little yellow stick-a-doo above the flashing light and continued recording. Jack stared at me for a few more seconds while I returned his stare, and then he proceeded to spell out his name.

"Have you had your deposition taken before?"

"Of course, I have, several times."

"Are you currently involved in any other lawsuits, besides this one?"

Blackwell grimaced for a moment before replying. "Yes, so what? We're a big company. Get on with your questions."

"Do you have a guess on how many lawsuits you are currently involved with?"

"I don't know. Several."

"More than ten?" David asked.

"Yes."

More than twenty-five?"

"Yes."

"More than one hundred?"

"Yes."

"More than five hundred lawsuits?"

"Probably," replied Blackwell with an angry toss of his head.

"Somewhere between five hundred and a thousand lawsuits?" David asked, trying to sound optimistic.

"Yes," replied Blackwell. "Can we move on to something else now?"

Everything proceeded along smoothly for a while until David asked him if he had completed high school.

"Of course, I've completed high school," an enraged Blackwell replied.

I wrote a quick stick-a-doo to David. *A little touchy there. Ask him as many questions about his education as you can.*

"Did you ever attend a junior college, trade school, or a university?"

"Yeah, what of it?"

"Will you please give us the names of the school or schools you attended and the dates encompassing the same?"

"Fuck you," replied Blackwell and sat back in his chair, fuming.

"Is that your total and complete answer, as to the schools you may or may not have attended," David asked with a concerned look on his face.

"Fuck you again---and again, you piece of shit," screamed Jack. He stood up abruptly from his chair, knocking it over. He turned and looked directly at the camera and pointed his finger. "In fact, you can tell those fucking judges in California that they can stick that fucking camera right up their fucking asses." By this time, he was almost foaming at his mouth. "You'll never see me in California, you bunch of liberal cock suckers!"

And with that, he stormed out of the room, slamming the door loudly, almost taking it off its hinges.

As Blackwell's counsel rushed from the room to check on the condition of their leader, David happily packed up his briefcase.

"Did you get all of that on tape?"

"Everything including the last three f-bombs and the slamming door," I replied.

***

The next afternoon we were back in California, sitting in the chambers of presiding Judge Emil Sorenson again, the same judge we had met with previously.

He watched the entire video without comment or any outward sign of surprise or emotion. After sitting in contemplation for a few moments, he busily scratched out a memo for the court clerk, who was sitting nearby.

"Gentlemen," he said softly. "I will be giving you a court order to serve on Mr. Blackwell in Texas. This order will instruct him to pay all of your expenses regarding his next deposition, as well as for those expenses that you have already incurred during your first deposition. Furthermore, he will be directed to answer any and all questions you might have for him, under severe penalty, if he does not comply. Please spend as much time there with him in Texas as you wish."

He stood and then showed us to the door. As David and Kiddrick passed by, Judge Sorenson pulled Kiddrick aside and whispered briefly in his ear. Benjamin laughed and said he would do his best.

In the hallway, Kiddrick told David that he would be handling the next deposition himself with Blackwell.

"The judge said that he could hardly wait to see the expression on the faces of the jury when they saw the tape. He told me to kick his ass," said Kiddrick, smiling broadly.

28

● ● ● ● ● ● ● ● ● ● ● ● ● ●

If it wasn't for Texas

Ten days later, Benjamin Kiddrick and I were headed back to Texas. During the flight, I showed him the magazine that contained the article about the video camera. He laughed at it for a moment and then went back to his notes. I continued reading the magazine.

I had brought up the subject of the camera with David without even finishing the article. Now I sat back and continued reading the article to its conclusion.

"Sorry to interrupt you, Ben," I said, after a few minutes---turning towards him in my seat. "But it says here, in the article about the video cameras, that we are allowed to use *two* cameras, instead of just one, in case one of the cameras doesn't record properly."

"Yeah, that's true," Ben replied.

"Well, you saw what happened when we used just one camera on him. We really need to order an extra camera. He might go completely nuts."

~ ~***~ ~

We set up the conference room just like before, with one exception. This time, Ben and I sat next to each other with a camera on either side of us. The opposing counsel suffered in silence as we made our final preparations before Blackwell entered the room.

I started both cameras the moment that Jack Blackwell entered and closed the door. He sat down across from us and immediately started swinging his head back and forth, between the two cameras, like a dashboard Madonna.

"What the fuck is going on here?" he barked. "You can't have two cameras going. That can't be legal."

His counsel stood up and motioned for Blackwell to follow him outside the room. They returned a few minutes later. No doubt, his counsel had reiterated his need to cooperate or face jail time. Blackwell now looked like he had regained his poise and was again in control of himself.

Ben introduced himself, reminded Blackwell that he was still under sworn oath, and started questioning him again about his education.

Jack remained composed for nearly thirty minutes until Ben changed the topic.

"Do you remember some of your past conversations with Sam Barns when. . ."

"No," replied Blackwell abruptly.

"Please, let me finish asking the question before you respond."

"Sorry," said Blackwell.

"Are you also sorry for not keeping any of your promises to Mr. Barns?"

"What promises? I don't even remember this asshole."

"Are you saying you've don't remember him, or that you never met him before?"

 Jack looked over at his counsel, who shook his head slightly.

"I meet thousands of people every year," he replied, looking smug. "Barns and his piss ant little company could easily slip through the cracks. The only thing I know about him is that he seems barely capable of running those fucking cameras for you."

"So what you are trying to tell us is that you don't recognize Mr. Barns, or even remember talking with him, even though he was President and CEO of one of your largest divisions at Southern? You might recall he was also on your Board of Directors."

"Please note in the record that I object to this line of questioning, and that counsel is trying to lead Mr. Blackwell," interjected his attorney.

"He was just one of the puppets running one of our operating divisions," Blackwell interrupted before another question could even be asked. "I tell them what to do, and they do it, no questions asked. If they can't follow my directions, we get rid of them. They are nothing. He was lucky to have a job in the first place."

While Blackwell was ranting, I left my chair, and without even being asked, very carefully placed yellow stick-a-doos over the red flashing lights, on each of the cameras, and then returned to my seat.

Blackwell went berserk. "That fucking asshole is nothing," he screamed. "Does he realize who he is screwing with? Southern will gross something in excess of $12 billion this year. We eat little people like him for breakfast. Fuck him and fuck anyone that has anything to do with him!"

Ben sat quietly, waiting for Blackwell to calm down. He was very close to totally losing it. Perhaps he needed another question to accomplish that. I scribbled a quick stick–a-doo and passed it quite openly to Ben. He glanced back at me with a questioning look. I just nodded my head as he shrugged his shoulders.

By now, Blackwell's attorneys had somewhat calmed him down, and he seemed to be aware of how his radical behavior could be detrimental to him in court.

Blackwell raised his hand and leaned in closer to his microphone. "I want to apologize for my outburst. I have been under a lot of stress lately, and quite frankly, I think it is getting to me." He looked over to his lead attorney, who gave him a solemn nod of his head and a mental well-done smile.

Ben looked at my note again and then proceeded to ask another question.

"I can well imagine how you could be under extreme stress right now. I heard in the news the other day about the torching of your beautiful Rolls Royce. Who wouldn't be stressed out after such an accident?"

Blackwell's face turned a bright red, and he abruptly stood up from the table, totally enraged. He knocked over his chair and flung his paperwork across the table towards us.

"Fuck you guys and fuck anything having to do with California. You still don't understand who you have been fucking with. Get out of Texas while you can, you cock suckers. I won't be responsible for anything that happens to you if you ever make the mistake of returning." He paused for a moment, still foaming at the mouth. "Oh, and just one more thing, tell the California court system and those fucking liberal judges they can stick their legal system right up their asses. They will never see me in California, so fuck'em!"

He stormed towards the large oak doors, flung them open and banged them hard against the adjacent walls, causing everything in the conference to shake for several moments.Everyone was very impressed.

~ ~***~ ~

On the plane back to San Diego, Ben couldn't stop smiling. "What was that nonsense about his car?"

"Just something I read about on the Internet. It must have been his favorite car."

Ben smiled and shook his head. "I've never looked more forward to a trial in my life," he laughed as he downed another drink.

29

● ● ● ● ● ● ● ● ● ● ● ● ● ● ●

There is no such thing
as an ex-marine?

Three weeks later, as I was attending one of the last depositions in Arizona with David, I received a phone call from my buddy Mickey Riley. He reported that he had just been up to my house in Fairbanks and that someone had set it on fire. No one had entered my house, but someone had piled brush up against the side of it and set it on fire. The local fire station was less than a mile away. It was put out almost immediately, and the damage was estimated to be less than $2000.

Two migrant workers were arrested a few minutes later, trying to exit the development. After some questioning, they admitted that a tall gringo had approached them to set the fire and had paid them $50 each to do the job.

I returned to San Diego a few hours later to check on my family. Jenny was a wreck. She had always felt safe in Fairbanks. I tried to tell her only the good news about our battles with Southern. She was unaware of me being attacked in Mississippi, and I always tried to put a positive spin on all of my deposition trips. She even smiled when I told her about Blackwell's antics in Texas. Someone trying to burn down our house was just too much for her to handle. I asked her again if she wanted me to try and make a settlement with Southern, but she simply shook her head and left the room.

I met with Mickey the following day for breakfast at Quimby's. As usual, the place was crowded and noisy.

I brought him up to date on the depositions and all of the people who had been bothering me. I told him the trial would be starting the following week, and then hopefully, it would soon be over.

I nodded my head towards the other side of the room. "Like that guy over there. He had lunch with me in Phoenix yesterday. Sat across the room from me, just like he's doing now. Never even looked over at me. I think he just wanted me to know he was around. I've seen him several times in the last four months at different airports, hotel lobbies, and even just walking down the street. Too bad, he wasn't the guy I hurt on my trip to Mississippi."

Mickey stared hard at the man and started getting out of his seat. "That asshole, I'm going to teach him some manners."

I reached out and grabbed Mickey's thick wrist and pulled him back. "I've tried dealing with this passive harassment before. He's not breaking any laws, and unless he overtly tries to attack me, it is just my words against his. It will be over soon enough. Just let him be."

Mickey sat back down, silently fuming, and we eventually finished our lunch. I paid the bill and then moved off towards the exit. As we passed the man's table, he looked up at me and smirked and then looked back down as he paid his bill.

I kept walking, but Mickey stopped at his table. He placed one of his meaty hands on the back of the man's neck and then leaned over and started talking to him as if he was whispering a secret in his ear. I noticed the tendons standing out on Mickey's arm as he continued to whisper quietly to the stricken man. With a final squeeze, the man slumped down in his chair, and Mickey joined me in the parking lot.

"What was that all about?"

Mickey shook his head and smiled. "Nothing much. I just explained to him that while you might be a gentleman and not mind assholes like him following you around all over the country---I wasn't a gentleman. I told him I was watching your back, and from here on out, and if I even thought he was anywhere near you, he could lose his head. I explained to him that I was with the Scout and Sniper Company of the 6th Marine Division, and I was sure that he wouldn't feel or hear a thing when

I removed his head from 600 yards out. I think he got the message. We'll see."

I laughed and slapped Mickey on his back. You really don't want to piss off an ex-marine.

30

● ● ● ● ● ● ● ● ● ● ● ● ● ● ●

San Diego Superior Court

We have all seen court trials on television and in the movies and can appreciate the drama involved in an exciting trial. Believe me, it is nothing like the real thing, especially when it's your butt on the line.

The first three days in court concerned jury selection, and it seemed to drag by slowly. I was amazed by the amount of effort that went into selecting a jury. We had hired a specialist on jury selection, and she had outlined for us what type of juror we needed to select to get a favorable verdict.

Southern's reasons for firing me, before my employment contract had expired, was initially based on three accusations, or charges, which were reflected in their counter-suit. The first of which was that I had an affair with one of my employees. This violated a "morals clause" of my employment agreement. The second accusation charged that I had mismanaged the company and that it was losing money rather than exceeding its sales and profit goals. And, thirdly, I was an alcoholic and chronic womanizer, and I wasn't even trying to fulfill my duties as a CEO or member of Southern's Board of Directors. Thus, I was deemed an embarrassment to the mighty Southern organization.

My lawsuit against Southern was based on the accusation that they had fired me without cause, thus violating a written employment contract, which in turn would save them (and cost me) millions of dollars.

Most trials, in the movies, have jury members who look well dressed and observant. This is not necessarily true in real life.

The trial was estimated to last approximately seven weeks. How many people could afford to take off that much time from work? The answer? Not many, only a select few.

The jury pool, for our purposes, consisted mostly of unemployed people, housewives, government employees, and retired military personnel. They would be required to judge the merits of sexual malfeasance in the workplace. They would hear more than a week of extensive accounting procedures and advanced banking techniques used by many Fortune 500 Companies and asked to make judgments as to whether or not the correct procedures had been adhered to. For an additional week or two, they would hear and judge testimony from several experts and numerous laymen as to their opinion as to how a publicly traded, Fortune 500 Company should be managed and operated.

If that did not sound difficult enough, they also had to receive all of this testimony at different times over the estimated seven weeks of trial. As an example, one expert, for the prosecution, might say a vehicle had six cylinders, and it was painted blue. Three weeks later, an opposing expert for the defense might testify that the same car was red and had eight cylinders. They were expected to remember this minutia and understand the significance of the differences.

I hate to sound discouraged, but I had a real fear that juror number 5, who was a fifty-year-old paperboy, may not be able to follow a lot of the advanced accounting. Juror number 13, who was a former nun, might be uncomfortable about discussing sexual malfeasance. A twenty-three-year-old, who was unemployed and recently released from the military, wore jeans, t-shirts, and tennis shoes to court each day. He had a high school education, and he was a former marine. We wanted him.

We started out with an original pool of more than fifty potential jurors, but the Judge quickly reduced that number, with a few pointed questions.

"How many of you have ever been fired from a job?" he asked.

Almost all of the jurors started fidgeting. The ones who didn't want to be on jury duty started waving their hands high into the air.

"Do any of you who are raising your hands, believe that you could not fairly judge the actions of the parties involved in this trial without showing some form of bias?"

Most of the hands continued to wave in the air. They were dismissed, and the juror pool re-filled.

It seemed as though almost everyone had been fired from a job at least once in their lives. The trick for Southern was to find those jurors who had been fired before but did not feel animosity towards a Fortune 500 Company who was trying to crush little ole me.

Both the plaintiff and the defense could also exclude jurors from the selection process.

Potential jurors were asked if they had ever been involved in a workplace romance. That seemed to make a whole bunch of people blush. They also were asked if they have ever been involved in an affair. Talk about squirming people.

They were asked if they had ever owned their own business. Have they ever worked for a public company before? Did they own any stock? If so, did they ever own Southern stock? Have they ever lost money in the stock market?

Because I was a real estate broker, that opened another line of questions. Southern would ask if the juror had a real estate license or if they had any friends or relatives who did. What a ridiculous question.

A joke going around California at the time was the story about the policeman pulling over a car for a speeding violation. He asks the driver for her real estate license. The punchline being, not everyone has a driver's license.

Anything asked by Southern of a juror that might be considered questionable was questioned in more detail, and if need be, they would dismiss the juror. That is why the jury selection took a full three days.

The final jury was selected, and a couple of alternates were agreed upon, and all were seated.

The demographics of this group were a primary concern to both sides.

Most of the jurors earned less than $40,000 per year, and many of them did not even earn a minimum wage. How would they approach and support a multimillion-dollar judgment? Would they determine that $1 million was more money than they would ever see in a lifetime, and conclude that it was more than enough compensation for a defendant who, in their opinion, was already rich? Would they believe I was just a little guy trying to steal from a well-known Fortune 500 Company and should receive nothing?

I was very uneasy after the final juror was selected. I had absolutely no confidence in how they would judge the case.

For the record, the newspaper boy was selected along with the former marine. Several older ladies in their sixties were included. Three municipal employees, one mailman, a nurse, a retired golfer, and an unemployed man in his forties made up the final jury.

Some early good news was that the judge, the Honorable Leo J. Thompson, who had been assigned to our trial and agreed to by the opposition, was considered a very good judge and was considered by the legal community to be above reproach. At least we had a chance at a level playing field.

31

. . . .

A courtroom – Dog and pony show

It was the morning of the first day of trial, and Jenny and I arrived at the Kiddrick offices for a final briefing before we were to walk over to the courthouse.

It was decided by all that Jenny would sit directly behind me, at the plaintiff's table, throughout the trial. The thought being that the jury would appreciate the fact that I had a beautiful, loving wife who supported and believed in me, and she was helping protect me from the monster Southern.

I started out by voicing my concerns to Benjamin and David about the quality of the jurors.

"How are they going to understand any of the accounting necessary for running a public company?"

Benjamin looked unconcerned for a moment before he attempted a reply. "This is probably going to go against everything you have ever heard about the judicial system, but I have found it in practice to be the truth, time, and time again." He shrugged his shoulders and looked over at David as if they had discussed this very topic several times in the past.

"They need to hear it, Ben," David said with a shrug of his shoulders.

Benjamin leaned back in his chair and took another sip of his coffee. He squared his shoulders and nodded his head as if acknowledging that it was time to tell me the truth.

"What I'm going to tell you is based on more than twenty years of legal courtroom experience. While it is mostly my opinion, I think you will find that it is very accurate as to facts and results. Here goes. . .

"The fact is, more than 95% of all lawsuits are settled before they ever reach the trial court. Of the remaining 5% that goes to trial, nearly all of them are *not* based on the facts of the trial itself. They are based on showmanship and perceived actions of the participants. Let me give you an example. Mary Jones is crossing the street in a crosswalk in downtown San Diego. She is run over by Fed Ex truck and is injured. Those are the facts. If left right there, Fed Ex would be at fault, and Mary would win a substantial settlement. In most cases, it would be settled out of court.

If I was representing Fed Ex, I would try and settle it out of court. The last thing I want is a badly injured Mary telling the jurors how her life has been ruined forever and that she will need millions of dollars to pay her enormous medical bills for the rest of her life. If Fed Ex convinced me that they were not at fault, I would still try to get them to settle out of court. If that was not acceptable, and I still wanted to represent my client, I would try to present to the court how Mary was irresponsible in her behavior. She was not actually in the crosswalk, in fact, she had been running at the time, and ran right in front of the truck. I would have three witnesses that thought they had seen Mary running in the area and that it was her habit to stupid things like that in the past." Benjamin paused for a moment and shook his head again. "I hate those kinds of cases. Nobody really wins."

David looked at his watch and then over to Benjamin. "Better tell them the rest."

"The jury will look at you, in fact, both of you, for your reactions, as far as the truth is concerned. In most cases, they will have trouble following the *facts* of your lawsuit. When there is an 'ah-ha' moment during the trial, where something major is said, the jurors will look at you for your reaction. If you have a minimal reaction, they will dismiss the importance of it. If you shake your head, they will hopefully understand that you do not agree with it, and it is incorrect or disputable information. They have to trust you almost from the beginning. If you can gain their trust, they will reward you with a winning verdict. You have to be aware that you are on stage throughout every minute of the trial, both in the court and out. If you wince at the wrong moment, they will assume you were at fault for something. Be aware, though, that every expression that you make has to be extremely subtle. If the judge notices you reacting in any way, he will call us on it, and it will be disastrous for you. Do not ever look at the jurors directly. Do not smile at them or frown at them or attempt to in any way to communicate with them. Don't be rude, of course. They are watching you. You do not want anyone to think you are sucking up to a jury member. If they see you laughing outside the courtroom, they might assume you are not taking this trial seriously. When the jurors see both of you together, they should see a loving couple trying to deal with a crisis.

"If you start to get on an elevator and you notice a juror already on board, do not get on---take the next one.

"When I present some of our exhibits, I will act like I'm sharing the Holy Grail with them. They will hopefully assume that whatever I tell them is the absolute truth. It is kind of like finding something on the Internet. If it is printed there, obviously, it has to be true. All of our exhibits will be the truth, and you will slightly smile and nod your head in agreement when they are submitted to the court. You will be watched for your reactions. While most of the members of the jury will not understand most if not any of the financial and accounting discussions, we will have an 'expert witness' on hand to explain it to them.

If they like this expert, they will believe most of what he tells them. If he is obnoxious and tries to talk over their heads, they will dismiss him and anything he says. In truth, it almost doesn't matter what he says as long as they like him, and he tells them his interpretation of the numbers in a favorable fashion. By the way, we have the very best financial expert on our side. He is a Ph.D. that teaches accounting at USC. His students love him. He makes debits and credits come alive and is very entertaining. We got him three days before our opposition tried to hire him." He paused, looked over at David again, and smiled.

"Another important thing to do in court is to continue your Post-It Notes---the stick-a-doos. You are the only one who knows everything that happened to your company. We might forget important points, or not see how they might tie in with the questioning. We have also found that the jury loves seeing a plaintiff that is involved in the trial. They will understand that you are not taking anything for granted. They will appreciate the fact that you are fighting for your beliefs and economic life.

"Well, now we know all about courtroom trials. I've got my puppy in my briefcase and David, you go get your pony and let's get over to the courtroom and get this dog and pony show started."

32

• • • • • • • • • • • • • • • •

Harvey Specter in the courthouse

As the Plaintiff, we are to present our side first before the jury. I was to be called as the first witness.

In truth, I have addressed numerous large groups of businessmen in the past. I have presented detailed project plans to community groups and to Boards of Supervisors in large cities. I have been interviewed a few times on local and national television.

I do not know what it was, but I was really nervous. It was everything I could do to try and look relaxed and confident in front of the jury. Just as soon as I thought I had everything under control, I noticed that my right foot was beating a fast staccato on the floor under the table.

I quickly stopped the runaway foot and immediately remembered that everything in my future was depending on how I was presenting myself in court starting today. At that point, I noticed that my left foot had started a new rapid staccato.

The chief bailiff called the court to order, and everyone rose as Judge Thompson entered the courtroom.

He spent a few seconds scanning the entire room before issuing a few brief instructions to the jury and the courtroom in general. He pounded his gavel once, and the trial began.

A relaxed-looking Benjamin Kiddricks stood and smiled as he walked over towards the jury. He couldn't look more confident if he tried. He smiled at a couple of the woman jurors and nodded his head briefly towards one of the men. In return, they rewarded him with smiles. He was making friends.

"Hello, ladies and gentlemen of the jury. I want to be the first to congratulate you on being selected for this jury. The last three days were difficult for all of us. To have a completely fair trial, for both parties, it is necessary to select jurors who are intelligent, unbiased, compassionate, and just downright honest individuals. I am happy with our selection.

"This is not to be considered a capital crimes trial, meaning that the parties involved here will not, or could not be subject to the death penalty should they be found at fault," Kiddrick smiled as though everyone could understand that.

"I would like you to treat this trial, though, with the same seriousness that would be expected of you if this were a capital trial. At times, you will be asked to try and follow experts explaining important rules or definitions of accounting. I don't know about you, but I find accounting very difficult to understand. That's one of the reasons I decided to become an attorney.

Laughter from the jury.

"To the parties involved, though, this could very likely be considered a life or death situation to them. It could mean economic ruin, social ruin, and loss of health to a severe degree. I am sure that you will pay close attention to all that goes on in this courtroom. You will evaluate all of the testimony and all of the witnesses, and then you will determine who is telling the truth. You will make your ultimate decision based on those truths.

"Some people have commented that this is going to be a trial somewhat like the battle between David vs. Goliath. The huge Fortune 500 Company versus a single individual, Sam Barns. When I talked to Sam about this scenario, he reminded me that it did not matter the size of the parties involved in this dispute. He told me that the truth was the truth, and he was confident that when everyone in this courtroom hears the absolute truth, justice will prevail.

"There will also be testimony about business practices and claims of sexual malfeasance.

"For those of you who have never been on a jury before, or perhaps might not have a strong background in business or accounting, I am here to assure you that if you pay close attention to the parties in this trial, you will recognize the truth when you hear it. You can recognize right from wrong and the truth from the lies. This is your opportunity to shine, and I am delighted you were chosen and are exercising your civic duty. We appreciate your time and your close consideration during this trial."

It was apparent that the jury almost started to clap their hands as Kiddrick completed his opening comments. They quickly realized that it was not appropriate and waited calmly for the opposing counsel to be introduced and hear his remarks.

The first surprise for me was the opposing counsel or lead attorney. After nearly four years of shuffling papers back and forth across the country as well as close to a hundred depositions, this was the first time I had seen the face of the enemy. This attorney had not attended even one event during all those years. He had been hired two months ago, and Kiddricks had referred to him as a "face man."

When I first noticed him in the courtroom crowd, I thought that he was a television personality. He had a perfect face, perfect tan, perfect hair, perfect voice, and was wearing a suit worth at least $10,000.

I wrote a quick Sticky Doo and shoved it over in front of Kiddricks. *It looks like Harvey Specter, from Suits, has a brother in the business.*

Kiddrick looked as though he was paying close attention, as opposing counsel approached the jury. He scribbled a quick note and passed it back over to me. *Discovery took so long that Perry Mason had to send in his regrets.0*

"Hello, ladies and gentlemen of the jury my name is Hughes Bentley and I will be representing Southern Industries during this trial."

My first two thoughts were: *Beware of slick-looking attorneys with two last names. Would the jury notice what a buffoon this guy was?*

I sneaked a look at the jury while they had their eyes glued on Bentley. I saw at least two of the jurors check out his suit from head to toe and then grimace. They may not have been impressed with his Harvard tie or his Gucci loafers, but I assure you I was impressed and nervous.

I zoned back into Bentley as he thanked the jury for their attention and looked forward to their fair play. What?

He rubbed his hands together vigorously as he returned to his table---his crowded table with eight attorneys representing Goliath. Not a very smart move. It made me look like Butch Cassidy facing the entire Mexican army with a slingshot.

33

• • • • • • • • • • • • • •

Show Time

"The Plaintiff calls Sam Barns," intoned Kiddricks.

My associates back at Fairbanks Ranch Realty would have called this "showtime."

As every eye in the courtroom swiveled towards me, I rose from my chair and tried not to trip, stumble or fall, while making my way from the counsel table to the witness dock.

I was supposed to convince my audience of my calmness. I spent an extra few seconds adjusting the position of the microphone until it was comfortable. Kiddrick had warned me in advance not to look nervous, or move too fast. He wanted me to be cool, calm, and honest.

Kiddrick asked me, in a friendly manner, if I was ready to answer a few questions, and I nodded my head, and answered clearly, "yes," that I was.

He spent the rest of the day asking me general questions about myself. We went over my work history, education, family life, and other pointed questions to help me appear more personable to the jury. I was making friends.

We broke for an hour and a half lunch break and then resumed questions until Judge Thompson called it a day at around 4 p.m.

I felt absolutely drained. Even though I knew what questions were going to be asked when Kiddrick asked me a question and waited for my response---they all seemed like they were shot from a gun. Jenny seemed every bit as exhausted as I was, even though she was only *watching* from a row back.

The plaintiff's team headed back to Kiddrick's office, where we spent the next three hours preparing for the following day.

At around 7:30 P.M., Jenny and I said our goodbyes and headed down to the underground garage to get our car. When we exited the elevator, the surrounding area seemed exceptionally dark. It looked as though at least two of the security lights had been broken, and there were pieces of glass scattered across the cement floor.

I felt Jenny tightly clutch my arm. She was aware of the possible danger too.

Of course, being in court all day, I had locked my little Heizer weapon in my car so that it wouldn't get me busted in the courtroom.

I told Jenny to stay by the elevator and hold the door open while I checked on our car. If there was any sign of trouble, I told her to jump in the elevator and head back up to Kiddrick's office and call for help.

I heard a bottle drop and scatter across the floor on the other side of the garage, and then the area returned to silence again. I was watching and listening carefully as I approached our car.

Jenny's Mercedes looked just fine, and there seemed to be no one around it. As I got closer, I noticed that the car was sitting much closer to the floor than usual.

All of the tires on the car had been slashed.

"Sam!" Jenny shouted.

I quickly ran back over to her and found her clinging to the door of the elevator.

"Are you all right? I heard that bottle break, and then I didn't hear anything from you."

"I'm fine, but your car is a mess. Let's go back up to Ben's office."

It was another two hours before we were done with the police and had arranged a tow truck from the Mercedes dealership.

As usual, Kiddrick advised that there was no evidence that our car had been trashed by anyone having to do with Southern. It might be possible that another low life, in San Diego, could be responsible.

And, I have a bridge in Brooklyn that I could sell you.

It was a quiet taxi ride home that night. We both were too exhausted to talk.

Back at our home in Fairbanks, we were relieved to find that it was safe and in one piece. Mikey and his nanny were asleep, and nothing was out of place or disturbed. We went to bed early.

The next morning when I awoke at 4:30 a.m. for my morning run, I found Jenny in the kitchen crying. I walked behind her chair and put my arms around her. As soon as I hugged her, she started crying even more.

"Are you going to be okay, Jen? Is there anything I can do to make you feel better? We're almost done with this lawsuit. Soon we won't need to worry about SI anymore."

"You could start thinking about your family more. I know you think that you are a big, tough marine and can handle anything, but Mikey and I can't. You keep daring these people to harm us, and they don't seem to be too concerned about hurting us. They are above the law." With that, she really began to cry.

I continued to hold her until the tears turned into deep breaths and half-suppressed sobs.

"I'm sorry, sweetie. I have been pursuing this lawsuit because I thought I was helping our family. I got caught up in the battle. I really didn't believe that our family was at risk. I'm sorry. I'll call Ben and see if he can pursue a quick settlement, and we can stop all of this?

She continued to cry and finally pushed herself out of my arms and stood up.

"I know you are doing this to help us, and I appreciate it. I'm acting like a hysterical mother right now. We need to fight these people. We have to stand up for what is right. That is the correct example for our son. I'm 100% behind you. I always am. Please remember that sometimes I may not as strong as you. I'm a woman and a mother, and I have every right to be terrified by what's going on right now. We depend on you."

A few moments later, I phoned Ralph Landers and arranged for him to provide security at the house until the end of the trial.

34

· · · · · · · · · · · · · ·

Superior Court – San Diego, CA

The next morning, the court was called to order, and Kiddrick resumed his questioning.

I spent two hours describing Leisure PT and how I had made it grow rapidly into a successful company. I explained that, at that point in time, the next logical business step, in my opinion, was to secure a strong financial partner so that we could continue our rapid growth and expand our markets.

After the lunch break, Kiddrick started asking me questions about Jack Blackwell, the president of Southern.

"How did you first meet or hear about Jack Blackwell and Southern Industries?"

"A magazine called *Luxury Resort Living* wrote a very nice article about Leisure Pathway Technologies. The industry referred to us as Leisure PT. It described our rapid growth and some of our innovative approaches to the travel industry, and it seemed to be well received by the general public. The following week we received several letters of interest from industry leaders."

"What do you mean letters of interest?"

I looked towards the jury as I answered. "Letters of Intent or LOIs are correspondence indicating that a party is interested in forming a business relationship with our company."

"Can you give us a couple of examples of from whom you received these LOIs?"

"Certainly. One example was United Resorts International, a publicly-traded NASDAQ company. Another example would be Southern Industries, a Fortune 500 Company, also publicly traded on the New York Stock Exchange."

"And what was the interest of these two parties?"

"They both wanted to acquire Leisure PT."

Kiddrick started walking around in front of the jury box and looked like he was deep in thought. "So are you testifying that Southern Industry was one of several parties interested in acquiring Leisure PT and that they contacted you after reading this article in the Resort magazine?"

"Yes, that is correct."

"Wow, that had to be really exciting for your company. Multiple public companies wanting to acquire you and take you to the next level." He paused for a moment as if shaking his head in wonder. "How in the world could you decide which company to choose?"

"Well, first, I had to meet with both of the companies to determine what they were willing to pay to complete our acquisition. After finding the current market value of my company, I had to determine which company was the most stable, and which one would ensure the best fit for our future success."

"And then what happened?"

"I met with the principals of those companies, along with their top management team, and tried to determine who could offer us the most value and security."

"And, after you completed this process, you selected Fortune 500 Company, Southern Industries---is that correct?"

"Yes, that is correct."

"Can you tell us who the primary person you met with at Southern---the person most instrumental in helping you make the decision to be acquired by Southern?"

"Yes. Jack Blackwell, the CEO and Chairman."

"How many times did you meet or talk with Jack Blackwell?"

"Several times, both in person and over the phone."

"And you made your decision to be acquired by Southern at least partially because of his assurances to you?"

"That is correct."

"What were some of your initial impressions of him?"

"I thought that he was exceptionally bright. He dressed better than anyone I had ever met before, with maybe the exception of Mr. Bentley, Southern's counsel. . ."

I paused for a moment as most of the jurors chuckled.

"He looked successful. He asked pointed questions about our operations and market potential. He seemed to actually listen to all of my responses and seemed to weigh them carefully."

At this point, Kiddrick seemed to go off our script and started asking questions that we had not discussed before.

"Looking back, was there anything about him that you didn't like?"

"Yes, everything I just mentioned. He was bright, smart, asked good questions, and then totally stabbed me in the back when he decided I was no longer of value to him. I trusted him, and then he fired me without cause to save his company, and his own pocket, millions of dollars."

Several jurors sucked in their breath quickly and looked surprised.

At that point, Kiddrick stated that he had no further questions for me, and turned it over to the defense counsel for cross-examination.

Judge Thompson stated that this would be a good time to break for lunch and dismissed the jurors.

35

• • • • • • • • • • • • • •

Howard Specter vs. Sam Barns

The jury looked energized as they returned from lunch. The testimony was getting exciting, and I think several of them could smell blood in the water.

Handsome, Hughes Bentley acted like a fighter getting ready to enter the ring. He stretched and shook out his arms and swiveled his neck muscles, and virtually did everything to get prepared, except put in a mouthpiece.

He strolled over towards the jury box and put $20,000 worth of veneers to good use. Kiddrick had explained to me that Bentley was a specialist attorney hired by Southern to question me and hopefully make a friendly, likable impression on the jury. He might not be the brightest bulb in the chandelier, but he was undoubtedly going to try and put a happy, friendly face on Goliath.

He reintroduced himself to the jury and then reluctantly broke himself away to spend a few moments trying to befriend me while adding bits of humor to his statements to help ingratiate himself with the jury.

When he felt that everyone in the courtroom was his buddy, he started his cross-examination.

During the next few days, he was planning to question me about everything I had ever done in my entire life.

In a movie, he would have received numerous objections, as to relevancy, and be ordered to "move on" by the judge. Benjamin would tell me each evening that I was doing great and that I was handling his questions correctly. He reminded me several times, to always listen to the complete question that was being addressed to me and then think about it for a moment before replying. He said that so far, Bentley had been kind and was playing softball, hoping that I would be lulled into making a mistake that he could then use to take advantage of me in front of the jury.

The next day he started asking me more pointed questions.

"Mr. Barns, I understand you traveled a lot with your job."

Do not answer if it is not a question, I reminded myself.

"Mr. Barns, I asked you a question, would you like me to repeat it?"

"Please do. I did not hear a question. I thought you were expressing an opinion."

"I believe your right," he smiled and shook his head innocently at the jury. They dutifully smiled back.

"Do you travel a lot in your job?"

"No."

"What? Did I hear you correctly? It was my impression that you traveled all over the world with your job. Didn't you acquire and work with resorts in foreign countries?"

"I did---yes, at one time. That was not what you asked me. You asked if I traveled a lot. Since I left Leisure PT, I don't."

"Are you employed at this time?"

"Yes."

"How are you employed?

"I sell real estate locally."

"Is that right? Can you give me just a moment? I don't remember reading that in your deposition papers."

Bentley made a show of finding my deposition papers, which were now almost the size of two large phone books, nearly two thousand pages, and shuffled through them until he came to a marked page.

"Okay, here it is," he announced. "Hmm, this is interesting. You testified under penalty of perjury that you were one of the top managers at Fairbanks Ranch, a large luxury subdivision in North County, San Diego. That sounds like a pretty posh job to me. Obviously, you didn't suffer any kind of severe financial or mental hardship there." He looked at me as if waiting for my response.

I waited patiently.

"Well, what do you have to say about that?"

"Sorry," I replied, "I wasn't aware that was a question?"

"Well, let me talk really slow so that maybe all of us in this courtroom can help me understand what I trying to get at." He looked over at the jurors and shook his head in fake confusion and then smiled. "When Southern presents their defense in this court trial, one of the main accusations that they have filed against you is that you were a terrible manager. You were not successful in growing the business, and quite frankly, you were a drunk."

I kept waiting for Kiddrick to object, but he just sat there in his chair with a slight smile on his face, making a few notations on his notepad.

Bentley stood in front of me with a disappointed look on his face.

"What do you have to say for yourself?"

Finally, Kiddrick stood and objected. "Your honor, I think we have all been very patient with Mr. Bentley. If he has a specific question or questions, could he just ask them rather than make this a guessing game?"

"Mr. Bentley, please ask specific questions so that we can end this session at a reasonable time today. Your brevity would be appreciated," said the judge.

Bentley bowed slightly towards the judge and then the jury. "Please accept my apologies. My enthusiasm got away from me when I noticed the large error in the testimony we just heard."

Mr. Bentley," the judge interrupted, "Just get on with your questions. You will have plenty of time during your closing arguments to editorialize your opinions. Now is not the proper time. I don't need to remind you of this, I'm sure."

"You are right, your honor. I apologize. I will finish up my cross-examination of Mr. Barns in just a few moments."

Bentley opened the deposition file again, found his place, and then resumed his questions.

"Mr. Barns. Are you familiar with the charges that were filed against you---and the stated reasons cited by Southern Industries for your firing as CEO of Leisure PT?"

"Yes."

"They cited that you were a terrible manager. Is that true?"

"Is it true that that was what they cited? Is that your question? Or do you mean, do I agree with their citing? I really don't understand what you're asking."

The jurors were starting to pay attention to this segment of questioning. A few of them were even chuckling at Bentley.

He smiled tightly at the jurors and then looked over at me. "I'm sure you understand what I mean, but let me try to be perfectly clear. The First question---Southern fired you and indicated you were a terrible manager for them. Were you a terrible manager?"

"No."

"You were a top executive at Fairbanks Ranch, and you no longer have that position. Is that an accurate statement?"

"Yes."

"According to your deposition you were earning $250,000 per year as a top executive with Fairbanks Ranch, is that correct?"

"Yes."

Bentley nodded his head and smiled at the jury before asking his next question. "I assume it would be safe for the court and me to assume that you are not making $250,000 per year in your current job. Is that correct?"

"Yes."

Everyone started talking among themselves in the courtroom, including the jurors.

The judge banged his gavel once and asked everyone to be quiet so that Bentley could continue his questions.

I just have one last question before I am through with Mr. Barns, your honor.

"Please proceed."

"Mr. Barns, you had testified that you often traveled all over the world when you were the CEO of the Leisure PT. What was your favorite drink while you were spending those long hours on plane trips?"

"Well, I know it's not supposed to be very good for you, but I drank it all the time regardless. Diet Coke."

"Not Johnny Walker Black Label, a dry vodka martini or tequila shots, but Diet Coke. Is that your testimony?"

"It is indeed," I replied.

"We are done with Mr. Barns, for the time being, your Honor, but we look forward to questioning him further when it is our turn to present evidence."

The judge looked over at Benjamin. "Mr. Kiddrick, would you like to ask any more questions of your client, or can it wait until tomorrow?"

Kiddrick got up and stood directly in front of me. "Just a couple of quick questions, and then we can all call it a day, your Honor if that is agreeable with you."

The judge motioned for him to proceed.

"Sam, I just want to clear up a couple of questions Mr. Bentley asked you, which might have been a bit confusing for everyone. You testified that you were a top executive at Fairbanks Ranch, and you earned approximately $250,000 per year. Is that a correct statement?"

"Yes, it is."

"Okay. Were you fired from that executive position?

"No."

"My impression is that everyone in this courtroom would love to know why you switched jobs at Fairbanks Ranch and went from a top executive to a real estate broker selling the property. Can you tell us your reasoning?"

"Sure, I would be happy to. When I was employed by Leisure PT, I worked an average of 60 to 80 hours per week. I worked seven days a week and traveled more than 25,000 miles per month on airlines all over the world. When I became an executive at Fairbanks, my typical workday started at 5 a.m. in the morning, and it often didn't end until after midnight---and again, I worked seven days a week.

"I observed how much money our own salespeople earned, and the hours required in their work. I watched them for more than a year, and I was quite envious. I requested to be transferred to sales and sales management."

"So you gave up earning $250,000 per year to earn *less* money, but in return, you could enjoy more free time?" asked Kiddricks.

"No, not exactly. Within my first four months of selling real estate at Fairbanks Ranch, I earned $350,000, and I have averaged about $80,000 per month since that time."

Kiddricks looked over at the jury before commenting. "Let me see if I understand this. You are making more than four times the amount now than you made as an executive at Fairbanks Ranch and working significantly fewer hours in doing so. I don't know if anyone could doubt your reasons for making such a change." He paused for a moment and looked again, pointedly at the jury. "By the way, how much did you earn as the CEO of Leisure PT when you worked for Southern?"

"About one-third of what I make today."

"And, Mr. Bentley indicated that you were considered a terrible, lazy, and incompetent manager by Southern Industries."

"Yes. That's what he said."

"I don't know if I could characterize anyone who worked 80 hour weeks as being lazy and if you were incompetent, how could you be so successful now?"

36

• • • • • • • • • • • • • • •

The expert witness

Professor Gene Hawkins was comfortable working before an audience of students who needed to be stimulated to pay attention. If he was too dry during his lectures, the students would tune him out, and it would be a wasted day for everyone. Fortunately, the professor could have been a success in several other occupations, including stand-up comedy.

Within minutes he had the courtroom almost in tears. They could not stop laughing, including the judge. During part of his testimony, he used a Powerpoint presentation to demonstrate how I had increased the revenues of Leisure PT from $0 to millions of dollars in just a few short months. He looked over at me for a moment and winked his eye and asked me if there were any job openings available at the Leisure PT. He said he could start work tomorrow.

When Bentley tried to object to this humor, the jurors actually looked at him with hatred in their eyes. He sat back down quickly, so as not to further inflame the jury.

By the time he was finished extrapolating what the future growth of Leisure PT could be, the jurors and *I* all wanted to work again at such a magnificent company, or at least the jury did. I certainly had second thoughts.

After Judge Thompson dismissed the jury, we returned to Kiddrick's office to try and prepare for the following day.

37

● ● ● ● ● ● ● ● ● ● ● ● ● ●

Phone sex

Hours later, after all of Kiddrick's associates had left for the day, David, Benjamin, Jenny, and I continued to review files that we thought may become pertinent in the following days.

The phone repeatedly rang at the reception desk, and David finally left our conference room to forward all calls to their answering service. He was gone for several minutes.

He re-entered the room with a concerned look on his face.

"Sam, can I speak to you for a minute out here?"

I followed him out of the room and into a nearby office.

"Do you know a Mary Stilo?"

I thought for a moment and then shook my head. "I don't think so. Should I?"

"I didn't want to discuss this with Jenny in the room. Do you remember sleeping with a woman named Mary Stilo?"

"What? Give me a break. Who is Mary Stilo?"

"Stilo is her married name. When she worked for you, her maiden name was Maryanne Brown."

"Maryann---sure. She used to be in charge of our new project accounts. I went on a lot of trips with her, but I certainly never slept with her. Is she accusing me of sleeping with her?"

"No, but Southern is, and she said it is ruining her life."

"Let's go back into the other room. I think everyone should hear this, including my wife."

"Better start at the beginning David," said Benjamin after we returned to the other room.

"A woman named Mary Stilo said that when Sam was fired, and Southern moved Leisure PT back to Mississippi, she refused to go, and stayed on here in San Diego. A year later, she married her husband, Davis Stilo, and moved to the east coast with him.

"They have a resort marketing and promotions company. They provide incentives for people to visit new resorts all over the world." He paused for a moment and smiled. "Guess who their biggest client is? Southern Industries."

I looked over at Benjamin and shrugged my shoulders. "What does that have to do with anything?"

"And?" asked Benjamin.

"And, now they are threatening her and her husband. If she doesn't testify in their favor, SI will cancel all of their business with them. She has to testify that you two had a long-running affair, or they will lose several million dollars in revenue from Southern. It is straight blackmail."

"What are they going to do?" asked Benjamin.

"That's why they called. They're caught between a rock and a hard place. They have no idea what to do."

"Let's talk to the judge in the morning and see what he suggests," said Benjamin.

~ ~***~ ~

Judge Thompson looked tired, behind his desk, as Benjamin and David brought him up to date concerning the threats to the Stilos. He didn't look surprised---he didn't look angry---he just looked tired.

"Do they realize that Southern doesn't have subpoena power to bring them back to California?"

"I advised them of that, judge, but that isn't their main concern. If Southern drops their account, they said they would suffer irreparable harm. They would be financially devastated."

"I think that you should explain to them the consequences of showing up here in San Diego and perjuring themselves in front of a jury. They could end up a lot worse off than losing a couple of million dollars in sales with the defendant. By the way, which of the attorneys from Southern approached them?"

"The Hamilton firm, representing Clem Garland and Western Resorts. Jim Hamilton himself," replied David.

"We have a three-day break from trial coming up. I want to make sure that the Stilos are not approached during that period of time. I think I will have a word with Mr. Hamilton," said the judge.

~ ~***~ ~

The following week, despite being warned by Judge Thompson to not contact or try to coerce the Stilos to perjure themselves in court---Hamilton arrived unexpectedly at the Stilo residence and banged on the door for several minutes until Maryanne reluctantly let him enter their home. He was abusive and threatening and promised to destroy several million dollars worth of contracts unless she and her husband testified favorably for Southern.

Maryanne called her husband at work, and fifteen minutes later, Hamilton was escorted out of their house, by the back of his neck, by an irate husband.

Upon his return to San Diego, Hamilton, and his associates were summoned to judge Thompson's chambers and sanctioned. The judge indicated to Hamilton that if the Stilos lost any Southern business in the next eighteen months, he would have Hamilton brought back to the court for further sanctions.

~ ~***~ ~

Kiddrick continued with the plaintiff's side of the case. It was a real fiasco.

Few of the witnesses remembered what they had sworn to in their depositions several months or even years earlier. The attorneys for Southern had requested that each of the witnesses re-read a copy of their depositions a few times before the trial so that they would not forget key testimony.

After giving their initial deposition, each witness was supposed to re-read the transcript of their deposition and make any changes that they needed to clarify their sworn testimony. Most witnesses did not spend more than a few minutes reviewing their testimony before signing it and returning it to their attorney. Virtually none of them made any corrections to their testimony. Their time was too important to waste on matters that did not affect their own wallet.

Most witnesses believed they were being dragged into a lawsuit that did not affect them, and they just needed to make a slight effort to comply with the wishes of their employer. These witnesses could care less what the results of the trial would be, in fact, several of them were no longer employed by Southern, but they were required to attend the trial if they had been properly subpoenaed. Without a horse in this race, several of the witnesses just wanted to get their testimony completed so they could get back to their lives again.

Every time there was a conflicting statement, Kiddrick would pull out the original transcript and challenge them on their changed testimony. Since witnesses were not allowed in the courtroom while the other witnesses were testifying, they often contradicted each other. To the handful of jurors who were paying attention, they would often chuckle or smile when there was a blatant conflict in the testimony. The jurors soon warmed to Kiddrick's humor, and it was apparent that they liked him.

Often, when one of the opposing witnesses would make one of these conflicting statements, Benjamin would raise up the transcript of the previous deposition and would ask them what answer they would like the courtroom to believe.

"In February, you testified under oath that Mr. Barns was a lazy drunk who chased the female employees around the office all the time and never got any work done. Do you remember saying that? It is right here in front of me. Would you like me to read it to you again to help you with your memory?" He paused, waiting for a response from the witness, and then looked over at the jurors and cocked one of his eyebrows in a doubtful expression. Looking over at the judge, he said, "your honor could we ask the court reporter to read back the witness's last statement, please?"

With a nod from the judge, the court reporter stopped her machine and read back the witnesses' last statement.

"Mr. McGuire was a terrible manager. He was never in the office. He was always out on the road working with all of the new projects he had brought on board for the company. He even missed our Christmas party because he was opening a new resort in Portugal. He could care less about those of us having to stay in the office."

Benjamin looked over at the jurors and then back again towards the witness. "So seriously, which statement do you want to go with?"

The following week Bentley presented the defense side for Southern Industries. He wasn't a very good attorney, in my opinion, but he sure looked good. Just ask him.

38

· · · · · · · · · · · · · ·

Deep Throat – San Diego

Late one night, after spending all day in the courtroom cross-examining witnesses, we received another unusual call in Kiddrick's office. A person who refused to identify himself told Benjamin that Randall Pate, my old shadow, had arrived in town that evening and was staying in room 614 at the Westgate Hotel.

This was very critical for us. They had been hiding Randall from us for three years. Since he did not live in California, we could not force him to come here and testify in court, *unless* we could serve him while he was visiting California. If we served him in California and he refused to show up, he could be sanctioned by the judge, which could consist of fines and jail time.

They probably needed him in town because they had been having trouble with the testimony of most of their witnesses.

Bentley had an attractive assistant who was tasked with prepping their witnesses before they had to testify in court each day. They were making ridiculous mistakes in court. Two of the witnesses, who had testified back to back with each other, said they had witnessed me being amorous with a tall, dark-haired woman, in a red dress, wearing stiletto high heels, who was also one of my employees. There was no break provided between the two witnesses when they testified. One of the witnesses was kept outside the courtroom in the hallway while the other was testifying so that they could not hear each other's statements.

The problem was that both witnesses described the same woman, wearing the same dress and the same stilettoes at two different parties, one being our Christmas party in Houston and the other being our New Year's Eve party in Mississippi. Unfortunately, neither one of these witnesses could remember the woman's name or where she worked within the company. They also didn't realize that I was in England during the dates of both parties, opening another resort for the company. When a third witness started testifying to the same information within minutes of the other testimony, Bentley requested a recess, for an early lunch, and it was granted.

After the lunch break, when the witness started testifying, she described the same woman again and then admitted she couldn't remember if she was wearing a red dress or a gold one and looked over to Bentley's assistant for guidance. Some of the crowd in court started to laugh, while many of the jurors started taking more notes.

The following day started out with a bang. We met with the judge before court started and told him it was our belief that Southern was hiding witnesses in local hotels for their benefit and not allowing us to have access to them. The judge asked for a list of anyone who we wanted to depose that might be in town. We had already presented the plaintiff's side, and Southern was almost through with their defense. It was not fair if they were hiding witnesses from us. In fact, it was illegal. Although the judge had not overtly acted in our favor, it was apparent that he was tired of the unscrupulous show being presented by the great Southern Industries.

Before ordering the seating of the jury, the judge requested a meeting with all of the attorneys in his chambers.

"Ladies and gentlemen, correct me if I am wrong, but I think we are just about ready for final arguments. I want to get your estimates of timing here." He looked over at the group of Southern attorneys. "How many more witnesses are you going to call?"

Bentley cleared his throat before answering. "We have one more witness this morning, and then we are planning on resting our case."

"Great. What is the name of this witness?

"A Miss Javits, I believe."

"And that will be all from the defense, correct?"

"Yes, your honor, that is correct."

The judge motioned to Kiddrick. "We all realize that you have been at a disadvantage because so many of the possible witnesses are from outside the state of California. Do you still have any witnesses that you would like to testify before we go to final arguments?"

Benjamin pretended to think for a moment then studied note from his pocket for a moment. "Your Honor, there were four people we really wanted to have testify in the trial, but we were told that they were unavailable and unable to be served outside of California. They are Jack Blackwell, Tony Stevens, Marge Collins, and Randall Pate. None of them have responded to our subpoena requests."

The judge looked over at Bentley. "Do you have any ability to supply any of these witnesses for the plaintiffs?"

Bentley shook his head in dismay. "I'm sorry your honor, but we have tried to provide witnesses for the plaintiffs, but it has just not been possible."

"You did your best counselor?"

"We did your honor."

"Alright, everybody. Thank you for your time.

~ ~***~ ~

246

Fifteen minutes later, after the jurors were seated and the court was in session, two U.S. Marshalls knocked on the door of room 614 at the Westgate Hotel. Randall Pate opened the door and was served a subpoena to appear in court at 1 p.m. that the very same day. The Marshalls explained that they would wait for him and escort him over to the courtroom at 12:45 p.m.

39

• • • • • • • • • • • • • •

The Kentucky Fried Colonel returns

Miss Javits was the final witness for the defense. She testified that she was in England over the Christmas Holidays in question, at the new London Resort and Spa and was helping the management get the resort open before the New Year. She said she saw me there with a Southern employee, and it looked like I could not take my hands off of her. Some of the spectators who had been following the trial started laughing and chuckling halfway through her comments.

Bentley jumped to his feet. "Your Honor, permission to approach the bench?"

"Granted," replied Judge Thompson with a slightly annoyed look.

Bentley approached the bench and spent several minutes in a hushed conversation with the Judge. He made gestures towards the jurors several times.

Judge Thompson looked over towards our table. "Mr. Kiddricks, can you join us?"

All three of them spent several minutes arguing back and forth before the Judge decisively nodded his head. When Ben returned to our table, he said that we had a problem.

The judge rapped his gavel. "We are going to break early for lunch today. I would like you all to return and be ready to resume your duties at 1 p.m. I would like Mr. Meadows and alternate juror number 1 to remain seated. The rest of you are dismissed."

A silence remained over the courtroom as the jury left the room. The two remaining jurors looked confused.

"Mr. Meadows it has been brought to my attention that you have been resting your eyes, or downright sleeping during the testimony. Is that correct, sir?"

Meadows looked amazed but hung his head before replying. "A just got a new job this past week. A night job. I'm sorry, but I can't keep my eyes open sometimes."

"We are sorry too, Mr. Meadows. But I am sure that you can understand the necessity of being an active member of this jury panel. It is not fair to either party if you are not able to keep up with the testimony. Is this a temporary job, or is this a job that requires your daily attendance?"

"I need to be there every night. I'm sorry, everyone, but I really am broke. I need this job. I'm sorry I let you down."

Judge Thompson nodded his head and hit his gavel once. "Mr. Meadows, you are being relieved of your duty, and you will be replaced by Mrs. Hopkins, alternate juror number one. Mrs. Hopkins, have you been following the testimony and are agreeable to assume an active position on the jury as a replacement?"

"Yes, your Honor. I have been paying close attention, and I look forward to serving.

I could feel a headache coming, and my stomach felt hollow. Mr. Meadows was the former marine whom I had mentioned earlier. He was the one member of the jury who I felt was entirely on our side. Mrs. Hopkins was the nurse I had previously mentioned, and the one juror who I had personally requested to not be on the panel. There was a decided coolness about her that seemed out of place.

40

. . . .

A disgruntled Colonel

When everyone returned from the lunch break, Ben started his cross exam of the previous witness.

"Miss Javits, I just have one question for you. Are you ready for it?

"Yes, please go ahead."

"What color dress was Mr. Barn's date wearing? Was it red, or was it gold? We have heard so many descriptions of this outfit, I hope someone has the correct answer." He paused for a moment as people started laughing. "You know, never mind. It's just not that important. I have no further questions."

Our surprise witness, Randall Pate, was scheduled to appear next. The primary purpose of Randall's summons to court was to discredit the legal team representing Southern. The judge would sanction them as soon as Randall entered the courtroom. I really could not think of anything of value that Randall could say that would either help or hindered our case at this point. He was the one key witness who we did not depose during our year-long string of depositions. He was always out of state---whatever state we were in. We could never catch up to him with a subpoena.

The opposing counsel had been previously sanctioned twice during the seven-week trial for various forms of misconduct, including the Stilos. This third time should really hurt.

The plan was to roll right into Benjamin's final argument after we were finished with Randall's testimony. The jurors could think about his comments all night long before hearing Southern's rebuttal the following day.

David and I had set up several special exhibits that Benjamin planned to use during his final argument, over the lunch hour. We were clipping cover sheets over the exhibits so they wouldn't be distracting while Randall was being deposed, but he arrived earlier than we expected. We never finished covering them all completely.

Looking better than ever, Randall entered the courtroom escorted by the two marshals. The jury had not been seated as yet, and it would be few more minutes before they were to be called.

The judge directed all the attorneys up to the bench in front of him. "Mr. Bentley, can you tell me who that gentleman is over there in the back row?"

Bentley looked towards the back row and nearly suffered a stroke. He had not noticed Randall when he slipped into the back of the courtroom. "I believe that is Mr. Pate, your Honor, and I don't really have a very good excuse as to why he is here in California. When you asked me this morning if I knew of his whereabouts, I was thinking about Jack Blackwell, not Mr. Pate, when I answered you. I am extremely sorry for this confusion."

For several minutes, the red-faced judge literally screamed at Bentley and the other defense attorneys. They were all sanctioned, regardless of what their involvement was with Pate. He then instructed them to return to their seats and directed that the jury be seated.

A few minutes later, Kiddrick was standing in front of a seated Randall Pate ready to begin his questioning.

"Mr. Pate, welcome to California. We are pleased that you were able to make it here in time before the trial ended."

Randall adjusted his microphone and softly said, "Thank you very much."

"Were you able to find a comfortable room in town?"

Randall perked up. "Yes, it's a beauty. It's called the Westgate, and it's really convenient. It's right up the street."

"Wonderful. We are glad that you are here. By the way, that is a beautiful suit that you're wearing. Is it English?"

"In fact, it is. I purchased it in the Mayfair District in London on Savile Row. *Gieves and Hawkes,* do you know them?"

"Actually, I don't, but I certainly appreciate their cut. Absolutely handsome."

At that moment, Bentley stood up from his seat to voice an objection but was quickly interrupted by the judge.

"Sit down, Mr. Bentley. I have heard enough from you to tide me over for a while. The plaintiffs have waited a long time for this opportunity to talk with Mr. Pate, and I'm sure you wouldn't want to interrupt anything they might have to say. Do I make myself clear, sir?"

Bentley, looking shaken, nodded his head and quickly returned to his seat.

"What was that Mr. Bentley, I didn't hear you?"

Bentley stood up and nodded his head emphatically. "Yes, your Honor, perfectly clear."

Kiddrick waited a moment until the judge motioned for him to continue with his questioning. "Sorry about the interruption Randall---may I call you Randall? I feel like I know you even though we have never met. Sam Barns has had nothing but kind words to say about you."

"You may call me Randall. Please do. And I have nothing but good things to say about Sam. It was a real shame that things went so badly with Southern Industries."

"Sam said that you two were almost like brothers. Traveling the globe 24/7, just about every day of the year."

"That's true. Those were really good times. I probably knew Sam better than anyone in the company. In fact, I know I did. You really find out what a person is made of when you travel with them extensively. Their strengths and weaknesses are hard to hide."

"Well, let me test you to see how well you know Sam then. Just for the fun of it. What was his favorite breakfast?"

"That's easy," Randall laughed. "He's always been kind of a fitness nut. He always ordered scrambled egg whites with a side of wheat toast---no butter and decaf coffee."

"You do know him. He still orders that same breakfast every time we get a chance to eat breakfast together. All right one more question before we get down to work here. What is his favorite drink? If anybody would know, you would, you traveled 25,000 miles or more per month with him."

"Randall laughed again. "What do you mean, *drink*? Everybody knows that Sam doesn't drink. Even though I tried to get him to a thousand times, Sam only drinks Diet Coke."

Benjamin waited for several moments while the testimony sunk in. "Diet Coke? You say he only drank Diet Coke? How can that be? Are you aware of the fact that there has been extensive testimony by Southern employees and management that Sam Barns is a drunk? In fact, a (he made quote marks in the air while saying the *keywords*) lazy, incompetent, terrible, womanizing drunk. Does this sound to you like an accurate description of Sam Barns?"

Randall shook his head and almost laughed out loud. "Not even close. Facts are facts. He doesn't drink, and I was with him almost daily for more than a year, so I know that to be a fact. And, if he was incompetent, how could he have contracted with all of those resorts worldwide and increased profits by nearly 1000%? And, finally, if he was a womanizer, he sure didn't share any of them with me.

Laughing throughout the courtroom

"If he slept four hours a night, I would be surprised. If he could fit in a woman during those hours, he should have been named CEO and Superman."

The crowd and the jury laughed along with Randall again.

During the past couple of days, the courtroom was getting more and more crowded, and I noticed that several reporters were also listening and taking extensive notes on the testimony.

Kiddrick was now on a roll with Randall. It was considered dangerous to ask a witness questions that you did not already know the answers to, but everything so far was working out like he was our witness, not theirs. So Kiddrick decided to continue on.

He waited until quiet had returned to the courtroom before continuing. "Randall, can you tell me if you are currently employed, and if so, by whom?"

Randall laughed. "I have been employed this week by Southern. They let me go a couple of years back when it looked to them like Sam was going to pursue this thing to court. They said that they would delay that process as long as possible. They said that they didn't need me anymore. I haven't heard a thing from them until recently. They said they wanted me to help prepare their witnesses."

"And did you get a chance to do that?"

"No, not really. The marshals came to my room first thing this morning and said that I was wanted in court.

So here I am." He looked past Kiddrick for a moment and chuckled.

"Something humorous, Randall?"

Randall motioned towards one of the exhibits placed just behind Kiddrick. It was a partially covered quote from Jack Blackwell. "When Mr. Blackwell told me to tell Sam that 'they eat little people like him for breakfast,' and then threatened him about fighting back, I told Mr. Blackwell that it was wrong and that he would regret it. That sign shows you just what they thought of his chances."

"So it was Jack Blackwell, CEO, and Chairman of Southern who actually made that comment, 'That they eat little people like Sam for breakfast?'"

"Yes, Mr. Blackwell himself."

"At an earlier deposition in Mississippi, employees indicated that you had witnessed Sam Barns and Mrs. Sharon Holt, sitting inappropriately together on a flight back from Southern's regional office. Could you describe this incident to the court?"

Randall nodded his head affirmatively. "Yes, of course, I can. Sam had brought his little public relations gal along with him on one of his trips back to Mississippi. It was Southern's opinion that if Sam had an act of sexual involvement with one of his employees, it would be a good enough excuse to justify terminating his contract. I advised them not to do that, but Mr. Blackwell suggested to me that if I wanted to keep my job, I should contribute to the storyline. At my age, it's not that easy to get a job anymore." Randall took a sip of water before he continued.

"Clem Garland set up a trip to try and get Sam and his marketing gal to visit with us in Mississippi, and then they would try and let nature take its place. We were going to try and get the home where they stayed covered with cameras, but it was ordered at the last minute, we had severe storms, and no one was available for the wiring job. So Clem told me what to say about the trip back to San Diego, which would be hard to dispute with me sitting right behind them. So I wrote out a statement about what happened on our flight back to San Diego. It was constructed and approved by Mr. Blackwell and Clem.

"They had me write that during the flight, no sooner had the aircraft left the ground, then Mrs. Holt had laid her head against Sam's shoulder, and they did just about everything but have sex in the seats in front of me---all the way back to San Diego."

More buzz in the courtroom. Those seated at the defense table were studiously trying to figure out how they had gotten involved in this fiasco.

"How, do you suppose, anyone would believe such a story---knowing you were sitting just behind them and could witness anything they did?"

Randall smiled for a moment before replying. "It was generally my practice, when flying, to have a drink or two after take-off and then go to sleep so that I would be well-rested for the following day. They suggested that I could say that I was sick during the flight and didn't get any sleep and witnessed them actually having sex together. You have to remember that they never thought that Sam would fight them this long. They were expecting him to roll over."

Kiddrick made a show of returning to his table and pulling out a file with several papers in it. He examined them as he walked back across the floor towards Randall.

"Do you remember what type of plane you flew on during that trip?"

Randall rolled his eyes dramatically and lifted his arms in hopelessness. "It's been a lot of years, counselor. How could I possibly remember that? I think it was a Delta flight. We almost always flew Delta because that's who Sam had all of the Leisure PT contracts with," he responded, looking pleased with himself.

Benjamin requested that the court place into evidence several documents.

He then held three ticket stubs in his hand and waved them in front of Randall. "You know one of the great things about computers is that they can save and retrieve just about anything. Take these tickets, for example. These are the actual ticket stubs you folks had from your return trip to San Diego. These stubs were recovered from your expense reports." He placed the tickets back in the folder and pulled out a colored chart. "By knowing the flight number, we were able to find out the exact airplane you used on your return trip. In my hand, here, I have a seating chart configuration for that exact type of aircraft."

Randall continued to look at him intently. He looked towards the defense table again and raised his shoulders as if to show his confusion and lack of understanding.

"We found something very interesting. The first-class seats in this aircraft have a very unusual seating configuration. The plane is usually used for transpacific flights. They require more space in the first class. Each row consists of two seats divided by a row and then another two seats. The seats are divided by a large comfortable table, which provides the passengers with the ultimate in privacy and space. It is barely possible for passengers to touch hands, let alone lay their heads on their companion's shoulder. To do anything more than that is almost physically impossible."

Randall shrugged his shoulders and slowly shook his head. He looked over at Bentley and chuckled.

"So you can see that it was physically impossible for them to do any of the things you mentioned in your written statement."

"I told them it wouldn't work," Randall mumbled.

"I beg your pardon, Randall. Please speak louder, so the court reporter can record your answer."

"I told them it wouldn't work. Do you think they would listen to me? They needed a reason to get rid of Sam, and I needed to keep my job. I don't even work for these bastards anymore. I'm sorry, Sam. I was ordered to say those things. It was just self-preservation."

"We appreciate your truthfulness, Randall. I have no further questions."

The judge looked over at Bentley. "Do you wish to cross-examine your witness, counsel?"

"No, thank you, your honor."

The judge postponed the final arguments to the following day and dismissed the jury.

41

• • • • • • • • • • • • • •

Jack in the Box

That evening after returning to Kiddrick's office, we received another call from our latest *Deep Throat*. He said that we should be ready for a surprise visit from Jack Blackwell himself in the morning. He suggested a few questions to ask Blackwell that would surely be difficult for him to answer. In past depositions, we had found out in the discovery process that Southern also owned a few banks and Saving & Loans. There were some reported irregularities involving the accounting. The bookkeeping was similar to what we had encountered at Leisure PT. The FBI was said to be involved in the investigations. *Deep Throat* sounded like he could be with the feds.

The next morning, when we arrived at the courthouse, there was a new sense of urgency in the air. Just outside the courtroom, the hallways were more crowded than ever.

I looked over at Benjamin. "What's going on? Why the crowds?"

He smiled back at me. "*Word* was probably spread last night about Randall's testimony. The press smells blood, and the rest of this crowd are some of the top trial attorneys from the area. They are here for the final arguments, and they might have been told that a famous CEO could be in court. This could be an exciting day."

I noticed the Southern attorneys and their paralegals were all crowded around a seated figure just outside the doors to the courtroom. Jack Blackwell was holding his own court.

Looking perfectly groomed in an $8,000 coal, black suit, he stared blankly into space, but I could tell he was listening intently, as the legal teams tried to bring him current with the latest results from yesterday's testimony.

Without breaking their stride, David handed Bentley subpoena papers for Blackwell, while Benjamin Kiddrick served copies of the same to Blackwell himself. "You've been served," they chorused together.

Without even looking at the paperwork, Blackwell dropped them on the floor and continued listening to the attorneys.

Bentley broke away from the group and approached us before entering the courtroom. "Mr. Blackwell has agreed to testify in court today. I will question him until noon, and then you can have him after that for as long as you need.

42

● ● ● ● ● ● ● ● ● ● ● ● ● ● ● ●

The Eagle has landed

The Judge directed the jury to be seated, and I watched their faces as they entered the courtroom. It was apparent from their expressions that they knew something was happening out of the ordinary. Most of them scanned the courtroom until they noticed Blackwell and his entourage, crowding the seats behind the Southern law teams. I could see them talking quietly among themselves until the judge ordered the court into session.

The judge requested Bentley to approach the bench. Soon after, Benjamin and David joined them. A spirited discussion took place. Not loud enough to understand the words, but it was apparent that Bentley was trying to glean some brownie points from the judge by indicating that he had convinced the CEO of Southern to fly to California and present himself to the court. Perhaps his hiding of Randall Pate could somehow be assuaged.

The attorneys returned to their respective tables, and Bentley walked to the front of the witness stand.

"Your honor, we would like to call as our witness, Mr. Jack Blackwell."

The jury, of course, had heard several weeks of witness testimony about Blackwell, previous to his visit today. While billionaires, like Bill Gates and Mark Zuckerberg, were iconic figures of the technology revolution, while Blackwell was the billionaire poster child of the hospitality industry. People often were in awe of billionaires, and Blackwell was no exception.

Every eye in the courtroom watched as Blackwell slowly made his way to the witness stand. He unbuttoned his suit coat, shot his sleeve cuffs, unconsciously brushed back some hair near his forehead, and then sat down.

He looked as though he was about to star in a Grey Poupon commercial.

He immediately poured himself a glass of water and took a small sip. It was apparent to everyone in the room that he was no stranger to a courtroom.

It was hard to imagine that this was the same Jack Blackwell that we had deposed twice in Houston. Maybe he only acted like a jackass when he was being filmed by an opposing party. We would find out in the afternoon when it was our turn.

"Mr. Blackwell, can you please tell the court your full name, and your responsibilities at Southern.

"Jack Blackwell," he said with a barely disguised smirk. "I am the Founder, CEO, and Chairman of the Board, of Southern Industries."

I was hoping that the next question Bentley would ask would be about Blackwell's education---now that could be exciting.

Instead, they played a polite game of softball for three hours, with nothing being asked that could hurt or bother Southern, or more importantly, challenge Blackwell.

Twice, the real Blackwell, who I knew, emerged, giving everyone a brief glimpse at his actual personality.

"Mr. Blackwell, can you tell the court how many conversations you had with Sam Barns while he was employed by Southern Industries?"

"No, I can't."

"Can you make a guess?"

"Not really. I don't really remember the guy that well. I have several thousand employees. I can't remember them all."

Bentley seemed a little concerned. "Do you see Mr. Barns here in the courtroom?"

Blackwell made a show of looking around the room until he finally found me seated, *right in front of him,* next to Benjamin and David at the opposing attorney's table. He stared at me with his cold, gray eyes, and I knew that every one of the jurors was watching both of us, waiting to see which of us would break away first. Under no circumstances could I turn away. I chose a point right between his eyes and concentrated on it as if my life was on the line. That probably was true, at least for my economic life.

After what seemed like five minutes, but was probably closer to 20 seconds, Bentley resumed his questions.

"So, do you remember Mr. Barns now?"

"Yeah, he looks familiar."

"How many times did you meet with him?"

"As I said before, I don't know. He was of little value to the corporation. He was just another body. What difference does it make?"

During his testimony, the jury watched me intently as I had scribbled more than a dozen Post-it notes to Kiddrick. He would read them quickly, and then put them into his own notes so that they would be ready to ask him during the cross-examination.

The Judge looked at his watch and then interrupted Bentley.

"We are approaching the lunch hour, Mr. Bentley. Can you tell me how much longer you will need with this witness?"

"I just have one more question, Your Honor."

"I'm not trying to rush you, Mr. Bentley. I am simply trying to determine if we should break now for lunch, or if you would like further time with Mr. Blackwell after lunch."

"I understand, Your Honor. Just one more question should do it, sir."

"Please proceed."

Bentley walked back and forth in front of Blackwell for a moment, as if deep in thought. He finally stopped and then looked searchingly at Blackwell.

"Sir, why are you here today? You manage one of the largest hospitality corporations in the world. You have more than 150,000 employees. Surely you have to be one of the busiest men we know. What has made this trip to California so important to you?"

Blackwell leaned back in his chair and nodded his head solemnly, with his eyes almost closed, before responding.

"A successful businessman can spend his entire career struggling to achieve his dreams. It is a difficult road to travel. It has many obstacles that must be overcome before any semblance of success can be attained." He paused for a moment, as if in deep reflection---or trying to remember his lines. "All of your dreams and successes can be crushed if, in the process, your reputation is destroyed by those people who are jealous of your success. My reputation has been deeply tarnished by recent events. I felt it was imperative to come to California to help set the record straight.

"A man is only as good as his reputation, and I felt that it was necessary to present the facts in person." He paused and took a sip of water and made a strange face as if he was stretching his jaw muscles, and then he re-arranged some of the hair on his forehead back to perfection.

Bentley moved over in front of him and began to talk, but before any words could be said, Blackwell raised up his hand in a motion for Bentley to stop.

A big mistake

"I'm not done yet. You heard a bunch of lies from Randall Pate yesterday. And, that was exactly what they were. He is a demented old man, who should have been put out to pasture years ago. He is one employee out of 150,000. Everything he said was a lie. As for Barns, he has lied since the day I hired him. When you have employees like him, you do not need enemies." He paused again and looked directly at me with a stare that could kill. "He is a little man looking for handouts. I had to work for my money, and he should too. There is no free lunch in American business.

"Speaking of lunches, I had lunch with Warren and Bill the other day, and we all agreed that it was extremely difficult being at the top..."

I noticed several of the jurors looking at each other and whispering, "Buffett? Gates?" and then frowning or rolling their eyes.

"There is only one way to go when you are at the top of your game, and that is down." He paused again as if trying to catch his breath. "Do you think everybody likes Warren? Nothing could be farther from the truth. He's got his enemies too. And, they lie. And with Bill, the same can be said. When you are at the top of your game, everybody wants to see you fail. That's why I am here today, to assure that you finally hear the truth, and put people like Pate and Barns back on the street where the bastards belong. I'm done."

43

• • • • • • • • • • • • • •

The Eagle has flown the coop

At 1:30 p.m. everyone was back in the courtroom. In fact, it was filled to capacity. Reporters standing on both sides of the room as well as along the entire back wall. Everyone was present except for Jack Blackwell, his entourage, and his attorney, Bentley.

The Judge took this all in for a moment. "Where is Mr. Bentley?"

The woman attorney, who had been preparing Southern's witnesses for trial, stood and addressed the judge.

"I am sorry, your Honor. On behalf of Mr. Bentley, he has asked me to explain to you that he might be a few minutes late. He is meeting with Mr. Blackwell, and they are running just a little behind at this time."

Just then, the doors to the courtroom opened and in rushed Bentley. "I'm sorry to be late your Honor. My client asked me to explain a few points of law to him, and he assured me he would be here in just a few more minutes."

The judge looked at the clock and indicated that he would continue the recess for another fifteen minutes before he called back in the jurors.

Benjamin Kiddricks left the courtroom but returned after only a few minutes. "Interesting," he said. "Guess who called me the minute we went on recess---*Deep Throat*. He said that Southern's private jet, with Jack Blackwell and his associates, cleared San Diego's airspace just a few minutes ago. I guess he decided to get out of town without having to answer any serious questions from us. That's not going to work very well for him, though," he said with a laugh.

The judge returned and met with all attorneys before to seating the jurors. The arguments went on for several minutes before Benjamin and David returned to their seats, barely suppressing their smiles.

The jurors were seated, and they looked disappointed. They were looking forward to hearing and seeing Blackwell spin his web in person.

As the court reconvened, we placed the large, professionally printed sign on the far wall opposite the jury. In bold letters, it read:

"WE EAT LITTLE PEOPLE LIKE SAM FOR BREAKFAST"

Jack Callahan, Chairman, President & CEO of Southern Industries

The Judge, who had previously viewed the videotape of Blackwell's depositions, instructed all children and the faint of heart, to leave the courtroom before watching a special video presentation.

No one left the courtroom.

A sixty-inch TV monitor was placed directly in front of the jury and another towards the courtroom.

Benjamin Kiddrick stood quietly in front of the jury until he knew he had their complete attention. "Since we were unable to cross-examine the CEO and Chairman of Southern Industries, the judge is allowing us to share his deposition with you via this recording. I am sure you will appreciate the difficulty we had in securing the correct answers for this trial. The following video will demonstrate the kind of cooperation we received from Southern Industries and their upper management while preparing for this trial."

Initially, there was silence as the video opened with Jack Blackwell entering the conference room in Houston, Texas. As Blackwell started swearing and refusing to answer the questions, noise and activity could be heard throughout the courtroom. Judge Thompson, at one point, banged his gavel sharply, demanding silence. After the first onset of F-bombs were launched by Blackwell, gasps could be heard throughout the courtroom. When Blackwell abruptly stood up from his chair and crashed through the doors to exit the conference, everyone in the courtroom started chattering out loud.

Again, Judge Thompson slammed down his gavel. "People, we are still in session here. If you continue to disrupt this courtroom, you will be required to leave. This is only part of the video I am allowing you to see today. If you can remain patient, we will continue with the video."

He waited for a few seconds until the room was absolutely silent. "You may continue Mr. kiddrick."

We were not allowed to comment on the order from the Superior Court, which allowed us to return to Houston for this second attempt at a deposition. I think virtually everyone understood the circumstances, as we all witnessed the inside of the conference room once again at Southern Industries.

The entire courtroom was holding their collective breaths as the deposition reconvened. Everyone knew that something explosive was going to happen again, and they did not want to miss it.

During the video, when I stood up and covered the blinking red lights on the video cameras, the cameras were only capable of viewing Blackwell, not me covering the lights. All of a sudden, he was going ballistic again. The jury, without exception, viewed him as a lunatic.

A few minutes later, Blackwell was composed again and apologizing for his outburst. I could see members of the jury and the courtroom at large, shaking their heads in disbelief. With a final salvo of f-bombs and the crashing of the conference room door, the screen turned to black. The lights were turned back on in the courtroom.

There was utter silence.

Ben walked over in front of the jury and shook his head solemnly. After a moment, he spoke. "If you don't mind, I still have a few comments to make to you before we are done with the plaintiff's side of the case."

44

● ● ● ● ● ● ● ● ● ● ● ● ● ●

The Scorpion & the Frog

After completing his final comments, Ben asked the jury if they would like to hear the story about the scorpion and the frog. Without waiting for a response, he began his story.

"Once upon a time, there was a traveling frog. He was a friendly frog, and everyone liked him. One day, he hopped up to a large river that he needed to cross. Just as he was about to step off the riverbank and into the water, a scorpion approached him and asked for a favor. 'Kind sir, I know that all frogs are considered great swimmers. You probably are aware that scorpions are not. We swim like a rock. I need to get to the other side of this great river before nightfall, and I am willing to reward you with a great sum of riches if you will just let me ride on your comfortable green back to the other side.' The friendly frog looked concerned for a moment, he knew that scorpions were deadly creatures that could destroy him with the slightest flick of their tail. He realized, though, that it would be crazy for the scorpion to sting him, for if the frog died, so would the scorpion. So, he agreed to help the scorpion and promised himself to be extra diligent of this danger after they reached the other side before they went their separate ways. The scorpion jumped on the frog's back, and they swam out into the river together, each depending on each other's good faith. Halfway across the river, the frog felt an incapacitating pain between his shoulder blades, and then he felt the stinging, deadly poison spreading rapidly through his body. 'Why would you do this to me? You are killing your own self in the process. When I die, you will drown. I don't understand why you would do this to both of us.'

"The scorpion took his last breath and prepared to die. 'It is just in my nature to behave this way,' he said, 'No matter what the cost.'"

Ben slowly stepped back from in front of the juror's box. He bowed his head for a moment before looking back up again.

"So what does it take to get the attention of a scorpion? From our little story, obviously, nothing seems to get their attention. But we are lucky this time because we are dealing with a publicly-traded company. What does it take to get the attention of a multi-billion-dollar public company? Does a fine of $100,000 get their attention? Obviously, not. That's chump change to a corporation of any size. How about a million dollars? That might pay for maybe a half dozen company limos---a small portion of their fleet. Would that make them shudder with fear and encourage them never to screw us over again in the future? Not very likely.

"No, it takes cash---and lots of negative publicity. Hit them in the pocketbook hard, and they will take notice. Southern Industry has reported revenues of more than $14 billion this past year. Their CEO, Mr. Blackwell, is a self-made billionaire. What does it take to get the attention of these billionaires so that they never behave like this again? We see it every day on the Internet. These multi-billion dollar companies taking advantage of everyone they can for the almighty bottom-line profit. Wouldn't it be nice to pass a message back to them? Let them know that we are tired of big business screwing us over, and we're not going to take this kind of treatment anymore.

"How many of you remember the movie Network?" He paused for a moment and looked around the courtroom and directly at the jurors. "I still remember one of the most memorable lines that made movie history. 'I'm mad as hell, and I'm not going to take this anymore.'" He paused again for a few seconds while his audience gave him their complete attention. "That movie first hit the theaters in 1976. That's more than 35 years ago. Did it make a difference? Obviously not. Large companies still act as though they answer to no one except their stockholders. No, that's not quite right. Big companies, like Southern Industries, only respond to their Chairman and CEO, Jack Blackwell. What does it take to get his attention? Obviously, he was too busy and too important to stick around here today and face our questions. We may never know what it takes to get his attention.

"Sam Barns and I are asking for your help. Let's send these crooks a message, a message that can be heard loud and clear. It is now in your hands to do so.

"We appreciate your attention throughout this lengthy trial and hope that you will send a stinging message to anyone who will listen. Please send a message, not only for those of us in this courtroom but perhaps for victims and potential victims, everywhere in our nation. They are looking towards you---and are hoping someone will help them. You have a unique opportunity to help everyone today with your actions.

"Thank you again for weighing the truth and for responsibly performing your duties, to the best of your abilities. Sam and I both thank you."

Bentley spent less than five minutes on his closing argument, and it was obvious that he wanted to end his speech as soon as possible.

The judge indicated that jury instructions would be handled first thing the following morning.

45

• • • • • • • • • • • • • •

In the hands of the jury

The following morning, as we entered the courthouse, Bentley and the other two lead attorneys motioned for Benjamin to join them in a brief discussion in the hallway. David, Jenny, and I continued into the courtroom and took our usual seats at the plaintiff's table.

A few minutes later, Benjamin joined us at the table and pushed some papers towards me. "These are from Southern Industries. They have graciously offered to settle the case before it goes to the jury. It is my duty to give you this offer and get your decision on it. They have offered you $1 million to end the trial today, right now."

"But they owe me several times more than that just on my employment contract," I replied.

"That's true. Bentley would be remiss in his duties not to make such an offer at this time. The advantage to you would be that you could get $1 million in the next few days and be done with this."

"And the disadvantage?" I asked.

"There are several. You might not be awarded anything if the jury believed the testimony of the more than twenty witnesses who testified against you. The jury also might feel that you already have more than enough money, and you should not need anymore.

"Remember we have jurors that are living off Social Security benefits of $1,200 per month. We have a paperboy who surely makes less than that. If the jury is not in your favor, you might be required to try this lawsuit all over again." He paused for a moment in thought. "Let's say you are successful. There is very little chance that Southern would pay you any of the monetary damages in a timely fashion. It might be years before you recover even a dime," said Kiddrick.

I looked over at Jenny, and she nodded her head. "We have come this far. I'm sure that most of the jury has the same impression of Blackwell that we do. I say we go for it. It would be a victory for everyone just to find them guilty in court. They might not pay for a long time, but it would give them a message not to try and do this with anybody else. This may be wishful thinking, but Jenny and I are willing to roll the dice."

Benjamin stepped over to Bentley's table and whispered in his ear. Bentley never even looked up from his paperwork and continued writing.

The jury was seated, and their instructions were explained to them for the next forty-five minutes or so. When there were no longer any questions, they were dismissed and directed to the secluded juror's room to begin deliberations.

~ ~***~ ~

Our team walked back across the street to Kiddrick's office and had lunch.

Four hours after we had left the courtroom, we received a call from the court that the jury was in. This wasn't expected. Because of all the technicalities of the accounting and financial claims, we expected at least another day of deliberations. Fours hours meant that there was very little deliberation.

We quickly walked back towards the courthouse, and we noticed that the jury had already left the courtroom and was walking out of the building, purposely avoiding looking in our direction. A sudden dread washed over me. After seven weeks together, we were almost close friends with the jury; they knew my life story. My first thought was that we had lost. I looked over at Jenny, and she looked terrified. She was reading the jurors the same me. When I looked over at Benjamin, he winked at me with a smile on his face.

"What's going on," I asked.

"You'll see---and I think you're going to love it," he replied.

In the hallway outside of the courtroom, the defense attorneys huddled together with their associates. To say they looked glum would be an understatement.

Benjamin smiled at them and nodded his head and continued on into the courtroom. The clerk handed him a copy of the jury instructions and their verdict.

Benjamin motioned for us to come over to a table and sit down with him.

"The jury has awarded you $28 million---so far," he paused, his eyes twinkling merrily. "They also found Southern guilty of sixteen counts of fraud and misconduct. The reason the jury didn't acknowledge us---is because they were instructed not to interact with us because they now have to determine the punitive damages involved in the case." He paused for a moment gathering his thoughts. "We submitted additional jury instructions to cover this possibility. What we have asked the jury to do---is come back with a dollar figure that will make a $14 billion corporation and its egocentric chairman take notice---and hopefully, demonstrate that this type of behavior will not be tolerated in our society."

Jenny and I were in shock as we drove home from Kiddrick's office that night. We were both silent, and then we would start to talk at the same time. Our minds were going a million miles a minute. I noticed a beautiful smile on her face. It was one of the first times in four years that Jenny seemed to be happy and vindicated.

In my review mirror, I watched a solo individual on a motorcycle follow us all the way home.

The bastard.

46

• • • • • • • • • • • • • •

Back for punitive damages

I didn't tell Jenny about the motorcyclist, so at least one of us slept soundly during the night. I spent the evening and following morning sitting in a comfortable chair in our living room with a loaded shotgun in my lap. At least it was a comfortable chair for the first couple of hours.

For the first time in months, Jenny was happy and talkative on our drive back down to San Diego.

With eight hours to kill during my vigil last night, I searched through my contact info and found the business card for deputy Busby again. He was the officer who we had worked with after Mikey's attempted kidnapping. At 1 a.m. I left a message on his voicemail about the verdict and the fact that the motorcyclist was again following me.

On the trip back down to the Kiddrick's office, I didn't see any sign of a motorcycle or a Sheriff's vehicle.

It was a different feeling in Kiddrick's office when we arrived. Ben and his staff were jubilant. Everyone was laughing and joking around, and very little work would be expected of anyone this day.

As we walked from Ben's office over towards the courtroom, it was an entirely new feeling. For the first time in months, I noticed all of the stores and offices we were passing. The streets were crowded with office workers trying not to spill their lattes as they raced towards their places of employment. They dodged around the numerous homeless, totally oblivious as to their fates.

We entered the courtroom without any fanfare, although there was a crowd of journalists just outside the door to the courtroom. While several members of the press shouted out questions at us and we could hear the multiple clicks of the cameras, we followed the instructions that Ben had shared with us before we had left his office and did not stop to answer any questions.

Judge Thompson entered the courtroom and directed that the jury be seated. As they filed into the courtroom we couldn't help but notice that several of them looked happy and excited. Several of them smiled broadly at us.

"I understand the jury has come to a unanimous decision as to the damages that they have agreed upon in the case of Barns vs. Southern Industries. May I have the documents, please?"

The jury foreman handed some paperwork to the clerk of the court, and she, in turn, gave the documents to the Judge.

The Judge read through the papers, raised his eyebrows slightly, and then adjusted his microphone. "Based on sixteen counts of fraud and misconduct, the jury finds for the plaintiff in the amount of $105 million. The total judgment in favor of the plaintiff is $133 million." The Judge organized his paperwork while the courtroom exploded in chaos. He waited a few moments for the crowd to settle down. He then looked over at the defense counsel table. "Do you wish to poll the jury, Mr. Bentley?" With a resigned expression on his face, Bentley shook his head. The Judge then looked over at the jury. "I want to thank the jury for doing an excellent job and for responsibly handling your duties. This court appreciates your time, commitment, and your careful consideration of all aspects of this case. You are hereby dismissed."

A few minutes later, Bentley came over to our table and dropped a piece of paper in front of Benjamin, who looked at it for less than a few seconds, and then pushed it down the table towards me. It was an offer to settle with the Southern giant for $3 million. I pushed it back towards Benjamin, and he folded it once before shaking his head toward Bentley.

47

· · · · · · · · · · · · · · ·

Finally, over--- right?

Many of the major newspapers in the country carried the result of the trial and verdict on their front pages. It was considered the largest court judgment award in California judicial history. One news station reported it was the 2nd largest award in U.S. history. It was second only to the Exxon Valdez oil spill---$287 million, plus punitive damages.

During the following two weeks, I received more than a dozen death threats via email and several more threats of bodily harm on my voicemail. We received miscellaneous calls throughout the night and finally had to change our home phone number. I turned all of this information over to the FBI. The experts were confident they had to be from people who were connected with Southern, but proving it in a court of law would involve another five-year adventure in the U.S. legal system.

Most people had a hard time understanding that what they had read in the newspapers, and viewed on the Internet, had nothing to do with reality.

Our family was just the same as any other family in Fairbanks Ranch. After the verdict, I didn't receive any cash. I did, though, receive hundreds of thousands of dollars in invoices and bills.

Jenny was not handling our successful trial very well. Her sister called and wanted to know if they could borrow just a couple of hundred thousand dollars to pay off their home. It would mean a lot to them.

A different home that Jenny had sold near the end of the trial was about to close escrow. The buyers wanted Jenny to provide their home loan, preferably at a rate at least a couple of points below what their bank was offering them. When Jenny tried to explain to them that we did not have the money as yet and we had no idea when we would receive it, they told her to get f##ked and canceled the escrow. Those and other such incidents just about destroyed her.

When deputy Busby stopped by the house and told her that they were not having any success tracking down the motorcyclist who was still following us, it was almost the final straw for her.

New friends and old relatives stuck out their hands and made their pleas for a piece of the $100 million-plus award. Everyone wanted their share.

Every real estate agent, who had a multi-million dollar listing in California, called to offer their services.

We even received a call at 2:30 A.M. one morning from an agent representing a mansion on the French Riviera. She thought her property would be a perfect fit for us.

After nearly four years of spending a significant amount of time with lawyers, I found that my legal education was not yet complete.

On television, the hero receives the large judgment, and in the next scene, he is observed driving a new sports car and living in a luxury villa on the beach in Malibu.

Not so in real life.

The system often contains surprises for the uninitiated. Southern was required to bond the verdict against them for an initial sum of $400 million. A few days after the verdict, the Judge recalled all parties into his courtroom. He said that after careful consideration, he was going to *remit* the award. That's legal talk for saying that even if the jury found the defendants guilty and awarded the plaintiff a considerable sum of money to cover his/her damages, it was up to the judge to determine whether or not the amount was reasonable and not indicative of a runaway jury. He said he also wanted to remove the possible threat of the entire verdict being thrown out by a higher court.

Jenny and I looked at each other in dread as we listened to Judge Thompson. Would we have to go through four more years of what we had just endured?

We couldn't do it. Of that, I was sure. Jenny started crying again, and I think that the Judge and other bystanders may have felt that she was being ungrateful for having to accept a lesser award, but that was not the case at all. This lawsuit had just about destroyed her life, and that of our family. The Judge was now indicating that we might have to do it all over again.

The Judge glanced a few times towards Jenny, and I could see that he was trying to rationalize for her what he was trying to do. He said that the alternative to re-trying the lawsuit was to accept the remitted amount. He said that he felt it was in everyone's best interest to accept the amount and move on with our lives.

The judgment was then remitted to $26 million. It was a lot better than a poke in the eye, but it still made me wonder why we rely on a jury system and then not follow through with their verdicts and awards.

We accepted the remitted award and thanked the Judge for his help, and we were ready to move on.

Don't get me wrong---we would have loved to receive the entire $133 million, who wouldn't? The possibility of going through another four years of this legal zoo would be too much to ask anyone.

The let down after the trial was tremendous. I had spent so many years fighting this battle that it had become more than just a legal dispute. It had become a way of life.

Again, on television and the movies, these things happen all the time. In real life, I had naively thought that cutthroat businessmen like these were just a figment of an author's imagination. I continued to underestimate Southern Industries.

Southern bonded the judgment at the new reduced amount of $26 million and then filed for a re-trial. Months went by---and then a year.

Benjamin Kiddrick needed to be retained again to handle the appeal process. I was again bleeding money and still had not been paid even one thin dime by Southern in five years.

I wasn't destitute because I was still selling real estate at Fairbanks Ranch. I was trying to support my family while earning enough money to continue my fight against Southern.

Jenny was not bouncing back as well, though. I was hoping that her real estate practice would help keep her mind off the devious Southern.

It didn't.

She let her real estate business decline and seemed to spend more time taking care of Mikey. She was convinced that we had not seen the last of Southern.

She was always waiting for the next shoe to drop---or the next kidnapping attempt. She started attending weekly sessions with a psychiatrist. Not with the nut job up north, who I had used previously, but a local doctor in nearby Solana Beach.

I had dropped out of real estate for nearly three months during the trial. I was now trying to get back into business again. New Clients were asking for me because I was a media celebrity in their eyes. Most of them wanted to look at homes, not buy. My existing clients thought there was no reason in the world I shouldn't reduce my commissions significantly, and some even suggested that I could help them for free or use my own money to joint venture with them. Life was becoming a big nightmare again.

48

It's time to settle

In the meantime, the California State Bar Association presented Benjamin Kiddrick with his third Litigator of the Year Award. With that award and the notoriety from the Southern trial, he and David had their pick of new clients from all over the country.

I called for another meeting with them to discuss our current status. I was advised that they had recently been approached by Southern to settle at a lesser amount than the final judgment. They said that they had told Southern to pound sand.

"I realize I told you months ago that we would fight them through the appeals, but I'm having a change of mind. This thing seems like it is never going to end. I have taken one gamble after another for the past several years. My wife is under a doctor's care now. She is certain that Southern is going to try and destroy our family even though the trial is over, and we are supposed to be going on with our lives. She is sure that our son is still going to be kidnapped every time he leaves our home. She is a nervous wreck.

"I don't want to wait any longer to get some money from these clowns. I want us to get on with our lives. I want you to contact them and find out what they are currently offering and then get back to me."

"Sam, you're making good money in real estate, and we have all the clients we can handle at Kiddrick now, what's the rush?"

"I just told you what the rush is. I have a family that's falling apart. I've been proceeding with this lawsuit for all of these years so that my family could relax a little and maybe enjoy life like normal families. It is not happening. It is no longer a challenge; it is a pain in the ass.

"I want to get out of this thing while there is still a chance of getting some of the award. From a business standpoint, the economy is in the toilet. The entire real estate market is turning into one big bubble and could crash at any moment. The banking systems in the U.S. could follow the real estate and also crash.

"I am sure you've heard the number one rule in business. *Pigs get fat, and hogs get slaughtered.* Let's get this thing settled.

For some reason, it took another three weeks before I heard any word from Kiddrick.

Southern's offer came in at almost half of what had been the original redacted awarded. I know that $13 million is a lot for money to anyone. But, I had to believe that Southern needed to pay me more than I needed to be paid.

Maybe I had read them wrong. I had put Southern on *Google Alert* and followed their news daily. Their stock was trading at an all-time low. It was now a penny stock. Fortunately, I had sold off all of my Southern shares on the day I had first filed my lawsuit against them. It was now trading at a fraction of that price. The New York Stock Exchange had already warned them that they were being considered for delisting.

Another dozen companies had won lawsuits against Southern since the notoriety of our award. They would never be able to pay off those awards. At least that was my opinion.

I told Benjamin to counter back at only $2 million less than the original judgment for a total of $24 million. He told me they would never accept that amount. I told him to try it again.

On Monday, Benjamin called me and said that, to his surprise, they had accepted my offer, their only concern was that the entire transaction would have to close and fund by Friday---just three days from now.

Just three more days and this mess would be over.

I was finally right about something. With Southern under extreme financial pressure, they couldn't afford to *not* settle with us. Because they had been forced to bond our judgment, they had more than $150 million tied up in our bond. They needed to settle up with us so they could have access to all those additional millions.

I sat in Kiddrick's offices on Friday, and at 4:46 P.M., the money was wired into our bank account. Jenny said for me to go to the office by myself because she was just too tired to leave our home.

I wrote a multi-million-dollar check to the Kiddrick law offices for their services, and on that same weekend, Jenny and I invited all of the jurors and their spouses to a special dinner at the Fairbanks Ranch Country Club. We thought it would be money well spent. To see Jenny smile again and be happy was worth any amount of money. The former members of the jury tried to talk with her, but she seemed withdrawn and tired.

Hopefully, we would finally be able to relax after all of these years of fighting the Southern giant.

49

· · · · · · · · · · · · · · ·

What a difference
a day or three makes

Those feelings of rest and relaxation all ended three days later on the following Monday. The headlines in the San Diego Union that morning indicated that Southern Industries had declared bankruptcy over the weekend. The article stated that our lawsuit against them had initiated a series of lawsuits against the former giant. To have any possibility of survival, they needed to declare bankruptcy and try to re-organize their company by renegotiating their debt.

Our payment from them had been in the bank for an entire two days.

My first thought was that it couldn't happen to a better company. I shared the information with Jenny, but she seemed to barely notice or react. I thought this news might be encouraging for her and make her feel better. If Southern was going to have to spend years in court re-organizing, they shouldn't have any extra time leftover to bother us. She just grimaced and returned to her bed.

The next morning I received a call from Ben Kiddrick. He said it was important for Jenny and me to come down to his office for an important discussion. When I asked him what it was, he indicated it would be best that he talked to us in person.

Jenny said she had enough Southern to last her a lifetime. She wanted me to go by myself.

Everyone was happy to see me when I arrived at Kiddrick's office. They should be happy to see me. I had just paid them several million dollars as part of their contingency fees.

As everyone congratulated me and smiled and laughed, I could see David and Ben waiting for me in their conference room. Ben looked up and motioned for me to enter.

They both looked uneasy as I entered the room. Ben shuffled the stack of papers in front of him as David made a few notations on a tablet.

"Hi Sam, where's Jenny? Was she unable to make it?" asked Ben.

"She has a few other things to do. I don't blame her. We are both so tired of hearing about anything to do with Southern. Anyway, what's up?"

Ben pulled out a sheath of papers and spread them out in front of him.

"I'm afraid I have some distressing news for you. This morning we were served with these papers. I'm sure you will be getting copies of these yourself in the next couple of days." He slid the top sheet across the table to me.

It is our understanding that you received a payment recently from the Debtor, Southern Industries, in the amount of $24 million. As this payment was made within ninety days of the date of the Debtor's filing of a bankruptcy petition, the payment to you is deemed a preferential payment and is avoidable. Please return this payment within ten days, or litigation will be commenced against you."

"If somebody is trying to play a joke on me, it's not funny. I can't begin to tell you how sick I am of this stuff."

"I'm afraid it is no joke, Sam. This is a real document from the bankruptcy court. They want the money that Southern just paid you back."

"Well, after five years of attending the school of legal hard knocks, they can pound sand. They can sue me for the next five years, or so, if they want. I can guarantee you they won't be able to find much of it should they win. The lousy bastards.

"Let them sue me. I'm starting to understand this whole litigation program finally. I've got the money, and they can't get it back until they have won it back in court. That may take years.

Ben raised one of his hands to stop me. "I know how you feel. I've got good news, bad news, and more good news. What do you want to hear first?"

"You might as well give it all to me. This entire deal ceased to be humorous years ago."

"The first good news, you have already figured out for yourself. You have the money now in your possession. You can use it to your heart's content. The bad news is that you need to hire a specialized law firm to handle this appeal process. This is a federal bankruptcy lawsuit. It will be expensive. Knowing Southern the way we do, they could run this through the appellate court system all the way to the Supreme Court, should they so desire. It could take years. The final good news is that we've got an ace up our sleeve that we think will work to our benefit. Follow this closely.

"Southern did not pay you your final settlement funds. Their bonding company paid you the money. The bonding company had the funds from Southern in their possession for more than a year. Therefore, in our opinion, the ninety-day preference rules do not apply to your case. As simple as it sounds, it still would be considered new case law. The payment by a bonding company has never been challenged before in bankruptcy court. While it provides us a good defense, it provides Southern a way to challenge the current laws regarding bankruptcy treatment. We've got a good defense team for you. They feel confident that we have got a strong case. But it will take time, and it will take money. This will take up none of your time but will cost you about $25,000 per month, to take this thing through the appellate process. You really don't have any choice in the matter."

I just shook my head in disgust. Now, I had to figure out how to keep this information from Jenny.

50

● ● ● ● ● ● ● ● ● ● ● ● ● ●

The Sam Barns Fan Club

Several months passed by. It became my practice to let the attorneys handle the appeal process, which pretty much depended on cross-filing paperwork against each other--- nothing more, nothing less, and of course, paying my attorney fees of approximately $25,000 per month.

Even though we now had enough money in the bank to feel comfortable, Jenny was still having trouble dealing with her hate of Southern Industries. It was as if they had invaded her life, causing her deep, mental anguish.

She was always on the lookout for Southern. Every time a strange car drove through the neighborhood, I would hear about it. She would sometimes call security several days in a row. She refused to leave our house, for any reason, after dark. I met with her psychiatrist several times to try and get an insight on what I could do to help her. He told me time, patience, and more therapy would be best.

I finally talked her into going on a family vacation to Maui. We stayed for ten days at the Grand Wailea Hotel. She finally started to relax during the last couple of days there. As we boarded the return flight to California, I could feel her tense up and climb back into her shell. She stayed in bed for several days after our return.

I started hitting the golf course again. I would hit hundreds of balls during lunchtime and then return to work. On weekends I would often play an early game of golf with friends or clients, and then I would bring Mikey back in the afternoon to play and try to teach him the game. We were even able to convince Jenny to join us. I thought the fresh air and the beautiful green landscape would help her forget Southern. It didn't seem to help.

One day while I was hitting some balls, the golf pro, Todd, came over to me with a gentleman in tow and introduced us. Todd said that the man, Jerry Hornsby, was a member of another affiliated golf club and was a scratch player and asked me if I would have time to play a few holes of golf with him and show him our course.

This happened from time to time, and I agreed that we could tee off right away. I did not have another appointment for the rest of the day.

We had an enjoyable round together and ended up in the men's grill having drinks together—--for me Diet Cokes and for the guest several bourbons, which he drank like water. He asked what I did for a living, and I told him I was in real estate.

"How about you?" I asked.

"Well, that's a good question," he said with a slurred voice. "Until recently, I was the GM of a resort in Aruba. You know, a really nice place. It has a championship golf course designed by Pete Dye, gambling---a luxury resort and spa with lots of women. A real paradise."

"What happened?"

"Oh, some asshole sued our parent company, Southern, Southern Industries. Now they need to sell off several of their properties just to stay in business. The son of a bitch put them into bankruptcy."

Gee, I wonder who the SOB was. "Jerry, that's terrible. Who was the guy who did this to Southern?"

With a big sigh, he finished off his drink and sat back in his seat. "I don't know his name. He managed one of our divisions called Leisure PT or something. Never met the guy, but if I did, I would put a bullet in him, the bastard. He ruined my life and the same for a lot of my friends."

I went into the locker room and took a shower and changed clothes. I was hoping to talk Jenny into going out to dinner tonight.

When I left the club and entered the parking lot, it was just starting to get dark. I was still driving my big, white Hummer.

Just as I started to open the car door, my cell phone rang, and I fumbled with my keys while trying to hang on to the phone. My phone crashed to the ground, and as I bent over to pick it up, I felt a hiss of air and a crash of broken glass, as a golf club broke the car window next to my head.

I spun around sideways and spotted Jerry Hornsby winding up for another drunken swing at my head. I quickly stepped inside of his swing, took the club away from him, and then gave him a short, hard punch to his solar plexus. He collapsed to the ground, and I made sure that he stayed there until the police arrived. I canceled dinner with Jenny that night because I didn't want her to find out about the attack. I would have my car window fixed first thing in the morning.

Add another name to the Sam Barns fan club roster.

Hornsby, later told the police that he knew who I was the entire time we played golf. He just wanted to see if I was *man enough* to admit it to him---so said the man who tried to take off my head with a golf club from behind.

A couple of weeks later, Jenny and I went with a group of friends to the Del Mar Race Track and enjoyed a day in the sun watching the horses run. Wow, that's almost poetic. It would have been a perfect day except for the fact that after the races, we went to dinner at *Pacifica Del Mar* to enjoy some seafood while watching a beautiful sunset that exploded across the sky in a blazing inferno of spectacular colors.

That wasn't the only blazing inferno.

I wasn't sure who all the people were at our table of twenty. We were out on the back deck with a hundred other people when a woman's voice screamed at me from the other end of our table.

"Are you Sam Barns? Are you? The same son of a bitch who ruined Southern Industries?"

All one hundred plus patrons out on the deck stopped their conversation and looked over at our table. You could hear a pin drop.

"Now that you have everyone in San Diego's attention, what do you want?" I said, trying to figure out who and what I was dealing with. She apparently had spent the day at the races sucking down every drink she could get her hands on. "You've got a problem with me?"

"Yeah, I've got a problem with you," she said as she threw down her silverware and tried to stand up. She had a male friend sitting with her who tried to grab her arm to get her to sit down again. She struck him in his face with her free arm as she tried to break out of his grasp. It seemed to only make him try harder to get her to sit down.

"Can you calmly tell everyone what your complaint is with me? I'm sure we would all like to get back to our food and drink. You've got our full attention."

She looked around the room and finally realized she was making a spectacle of herself. She sat back down in her chair and removed her arm from her friend's grasp. "I lost my job because of you. I was with them for ten years. Southern Industries, you do remember them, don't you? I was a manager. Your lawsuit drove us out of business. I've lost everything I had because of you."

"If you worked for them for ten years, you should have noticed that they were crooks and thieves. You should be thankful that you did not end up in jail like some of their other managers. They fired me too. The only difference between you and me is that I fought back. Can we all enjoy our meals now?"

Several of the people in the restaurant clapped their hands. The woman looked embarrassed and soon left the restaurant with her friend. Add another name to the Sam Barns fan club.

After the incident in the restaurant, Jenny stopped eating and just turned off. She was shaking by the time I got her down to my car. After that, she spent the next several days in bed.

A week later, Mikey and I played golf all day at Fairbanks Ranch Country Club. We were hoping to get Jenny up and moving around. Maybe the promise of another trip to Maui might do it.

When we got back to the house, Mikey ran to take a shower while I checked in with Jenny.

She was sleeping peacefully on her back, her head propped up by the pillows. She looked as young as she did when she graduated from college. I watched her a few moments and smiled. I could feel my heart fill with love for this beautiful woman.

Then I noticed the prescription bottle lying beside the bed---and the note.

I rushed over to her and put my face up close to hers. Her skin was cold to my touch. There was no pulse at her neck. My Jenny was dead.

I picked up the note she had written.

I'm sorry, Sam. I'm sorry, my sweet baby Mikey. I'm so tired. I just want to sleep forever. Love, Me.

51

• • • • • • • • • • • • • • •

It's all over

Six months later, the appeal process had reached the final appellate court in New Orleans, Louisiana. Southern had lost every ruling so far concerning the preferential payments. If New Orleans continued this process and ruled against Southern, they still could proceed to the final judicial step---The United States Supreme Court. It would take several more years if they decided to continue their fight to the highest court in the land.

At 7:15 A.M., I received a call from Benjamin. "Believe it or not, it's over," he said, with a happy-sounding voice. "As you know, the appellate court in New Orleans upheld our argument this past week. I just emailed you a copy of a legal document from Southern saying they were withdrawing their lawsuit. It is over Sam. I only wish that Jenny could have still been with us today. I think it would have made all of the difference in the world to her. I'm so sorry for you and Mikey to be without her company.

"It's time for you and your family to start enjoying your life again. Congratulations."

52

● ● ● ● ● ● ● ● ● ● ● ● ● ●

Some things need to change

I guess I am back to where I started…

I never finished my second cup of coffee. It got cold more than an hour ago. I either need a refill or a complete start over.

Today is a special day for me. It is February 14---Valentines Day. It was our anniversary date. It was also the day she died. I hate Valentines Day---do you blame me?

I'm sitting out in my backyard now, under the gazebo, waiting for the sun to come up. I have an aversion to running when it's dark outside. Whenever I have one of these sleepless nights, it reminds me of that guy on the beach in Biloxi. If he had been halfway smart, he would have just run up to me and shot me in the forehead. I would be dead and he would be relaxing somewhere with a bundle of cash, and maybe Jenny would still be alive. If only I could make that trade today.

Jenny. I've got to stop thinking about how I failed you.

Well, back to the asshole on the beach. I wonder where he is now. Does he have a leg that gives him trouble each day---I hope so.

I wonder if he gets splitting headaches from the hurt I put on him that night---I hope so.

I wonder if he is watching me right now through a night scope, mounted on a hunting rifle, just outside my property line, deep in the shadows---I hope not.

I think about these things all of the time.

The rays of the sun are just breaking over the horizon now. It is going to be another beautiful day in sunny California.

I hear the back-door slam as Mikey runs out of the house. He gives me a silly salute as he races by and continues running to the side of the pool before executing a perfect forward flip into the deep end. There is a big splash and then a bunch of bubbles before he surfaces and swims over to the side of the pool. In one movement, he jumps out onto the deck, and comes over to me to grab a towel.

I can see some of Jenny's features in him when he doesn't know I'm watching. Even though this is a bad day for me and my memories, I can't help but smile at him.

He is looking tall and on the thin side of lean. His birthday is tomorrow and he will be sixteen years old. We are leaving in the morning for a week or two on Maui, our favorite place in the world. We plan on playing every golf course on the island. I think Jenny would have enjoyed the trip.

I read on the Internet yesterday that Jack Blackwell has a new public company that he is running---which means, he is probably running it into the ground. Guys like him always seem to bounce back. I heard that he had been married and divorced a couple of times since the demise of Southern. Like many con men, he seems to have the lives of a cat. Well, good luck Jack, and good luck to anyone who has to do business with you. I certainly learned my lesson and paid a steep price for it.

I remember back during the final days of the trial, we kept pounding everyone with the question, "what does it take to get the attention of a company like Southern, or a man like Jack Blackwell?"

I think we got Southern's attention. But, Jack Blackwell? I doubt it. I'm sure he's the same guy, only with a different company now.

Like a scorpion, it is just in his nature to act the way he does.

About the Author

John E. Riddle was born and raised in Southern California. Unlike many of his favorite authors---none of whom he has ever met---he <u>does not have</u> a wife or one and a half lovable children at home, nor does he have a dog named Buster or a cat named Fluffy.

He received his academic education from San Diego State University, Pepperdine University, and UCLA. He served in the military as a Naval Aviator.

He received further heuristic education by pursuing several entrepreneurial opportunities encompassing---real estate, real estate development, securities, financial strategies, banking, education, medical technologies and has probably forgotten more than a handful of other unusual opportunities.

Since the Great Real Estate Crash of 2008, John became a prolific writer. He has completed six new novels with a few others waiting to be introduced in the not too distant future.

He does have multiple sons who are attempting to complete college, in between skiing, surfing, partying, and chasing girls (not necessarily in that order).

A Message from the Author

Thank you so much for reading **MORALS CLAUSE**. The original working title of this book was **True Fiction**---but it is a litigious world we live in.

How much of the book is fiction? I'll leave it up to the reader to determine for themselves. In this day of computers, it is amazing what you can find out just by doing a little bit of Googling.

I sure hope you enjoyed **Morals Clause**. If you did, please spend a few more seconds rating the book and writing a short review. Please click on the link below to enter your rating. Those gold star ratings mean everything to an author.

MORALS CLAUSE is the first book, in a two-book series. It is followed by **Red Ink**. Both books follow Sam Barns on some extraordinary ventures.

Website: https://www.johneriddle.com/

Additional books by John E. Riddle

Red Ink

How to Get to Heaven

How to Get In & Out of Hell

DOWNLOAD

The Third Straw.